Antoine Laurain was born in Paris and is a journalist, antiques collector and the author of five novels, including *The President's Hat*.

Emily Boyce is in-house translator at Gallic Books. She lives in London. She has previously co-translated *The President's Hat*.

Jane Aitken is a publisher and translator from the French.

The Red Notebook

The Red Notebook

Antoine Laurain

Translated from the French
by Emily Boyce and Jane Aitken

Gallic Books
London

A Gallic Book

First published in France as *La femme au carnet rouge* by Flammarion, 2014
Copyright © Flammarion, 2014
English translation copyright © Gallic Books 2015

First published in Great Britain in 2015 by Gallic Books,
59 Ebury Street, London, SW1W 0NZ

A CIP record for this book is available from the British Library
ISBN 978-1-908313-86-7

Typeset in Fournier MT by Gallic Books
Printed in the UK by CPI (CR0 4YY)

10

There is little but the sublime to help us through the ordinary in life.

Alain (Émile-Auguste Chartier)

The taxi had dropped her on the corner of the boulevard. She was barely fifty metres from home. The road was lit by streetlamps which gave the buildings an orange glow, but even so she was anxious, as she always was when she returned late at night. She looked behind her but she saw nobody. Light from the hotel opposite flooded the pavement between the two potted trees flanking its entrance. She stopped outside her door, unzipping her bag to retrieve her keys and security fob, and then everything happened very quickly.

A hand grabbed her bag strap, a hand that had come out of nowhere, belonging to a dark-haired man wearing a leather jacket. It took only a second for fear to travel through her veins all the way to her heart where it burst into an icy rain. She instinctively clung to her bag. The man pulled harder and when she held on, he put his hand over her face and shoved her head back into the metal door frame. She stumbled in shock, seeing stars that shimmered above the road like hovering fireflies; she felt a tightness in her chest and let go of the bag. The man smiled, the strap swirled through the air and he ran off. She leant back against the door, watching him disappear into the night. She was breathing heavily, her throat was on fire, her mouth dry, but her bottle of water was in the bag. She reached over and tapped in the entry code, put her weight against the door and slipped inside.

The glass and black-iron door provided a safety barrier between her and the outside world. She sat down carefully on the marble steps of the hallway and closed her eyes, waiting for her brain to calm down and start working normally again. Just as the safety signs are gradually switched off on an aeroplane, so the warning lights flashing in her head – I'm being attacked, I'm going to die, my bag's been stolen, I'm not hurt, I'm alive – disappeared one by one. She looked up at the rows of letter boxes and focused on the one bearing her name and floor number: 5th floor, left. But since she was without her keys at almost two o'clock in the morning, she realised she would not be going through the door of the left-hand flat on the fifth floor.

The implications of this realisation took shape in her mind: I can't get into my home and my bag's been stolen. It's gone and I'll never see it again. A part of her had been brutally torn away. She looked around as though willing the bag suddenly to materialise, wiping out the scene that had just taken place. But it definitely wasn't there. It would be streets away by now, snatched, flying on the man's arm as he ran; he would open it and inside he would find her keys, her identity card, her memories. Her entire life. She could feel tears welling. Her hands could not seem to stop shaking from fear, helplessness and anger, and the pain at the back of her head suddenly got sharper. When she raised her hand to where it hurt, she realised she was bleeding, but of course her tissues were in her handbag.

It was 1.58 a.m. She could not possibly knock on any of her neighbours' doors at that time of night. She couldn't even disturb the friendly man whose name she couldn't remember who worked in graphic novels and had just moved in on the second floor. The hotel seemed the only solution. The light in the hallway had just timed out and she felt for the switch. When the light came back on again, she felt mildly dizzy and had to steady herself against the wall. She needed to pull herself together and go and ask to spend the night at the hotel, explaining that she lived just across the road and would pay for the room the next day. She hoped the night porter would be sympathetic because she was struggling to think of an alternative.

She pulled open the heavy front door and shivered. Not from cold but from a vague sense of fear, as if the buildings lining the street had soaked up something of what had happened and the man might suddenly magically step out from a wall. Laure looked around. The road was empty. The man was clearly not coming back, but it was difficult to control her fear, and it's hard to distinguish between the irrational and the possible at almost two o'clock in the morning. She crossed the road and walked towards the hotel. Her instinct was to hold her bag close to her body but she found nothing but empty space between her hip and forearm. She stepped into the light under the hotel awning and the automatic door slid open. The grey-haired man at the desk looked up as she walked in.

He agreed to let her stay. He had been a little reluctant, but when Laure began taking off her gold bracelet to leave as security, he had raised his hand in surrender. The young woman was visibly distressed and almost certainly telling the truth; she seemed a trustworthy character and he judged the chances of her coming back to pay her bill at a good nine out of ten. She had left her name and address. Besides, the hotel had faced cases of non-payment that went well beyond a single night's stay for a lone woman who said she had been living opposite for the past fifteen years.

She might have phoned the friends at whose house she had spent the evening, but their number was in her phone. Since the advent of mobile phones, the only numbers Laure knew by heart were her own home and work numbers. The receptionist also suggested she call a locksmith but that too was impossible. Laure had used up her cheque book and had been slow to order a new one; she wouldn't receive it until early the following week. Other than her debit card and forty euros in cash, both of which were inside her wallet, she had no means of payment. It was remarkable how, in situations like this, all the tiny details that had seemed totally insignificant an hour before suddenly seemed to conspire against you. She followed the man into the lift, then along the corridor to room 52, which looked onto the street. He turned the light on, briefly pointed out the bathroom and handed her the key. She thanked him, promising once again to come back and pay as soon as possible the next day. The porter gave her a friendly smile, tiring a little of hearing the same promise for the fifth time. 'I believe you, Mademoiselle. Good night.'

Laure walked over to the window and parted the net curtains.

She could see straight across to where she lived. She had left the living-room lamp on and placed a chair in front of the part-opened window so that Belphégor could look out. It was very odd seeing her flat from here. She almost expected to glimpse herself crossing the room. She opened the window.

'Belphégor,' she called in a whisper, 'Belphégor,' making the sharp little kissing sound all cat owners can make.

A few moments later, the black shape leapt up onto the chair and two yellow eyes stared back at her in amazement. How on earth was it possible for his mistress to be across the road and not inside the flat?

'That's right, I'm over here,' she told him with a shrug.

She gave him a little wave and decided to get ready for bed. In the bathroom, she found a box of tissues and some water to clean the wound to her head. As she leant over, she felt dizzy again, but at least she seemed to have stopped bleeding. She took a towel and laid it over the pillow, and then she got undressed. Lying down, she could not stop replaying the scene of the mugging. The incident, which had lasted no more than a few seconds, was now developing into a slow-motion sequence. Longer and more fluid than the stylised sequences in films. More like the ones in science documentaries of dummies in simulated car crashes. You see the inside of the vehicle, the windscreen blowing out like a vertical puddle of water, the dummies' heads moving smoothly forward, the airbags inflating like bubble gum and the metal shell lightly crumpling, as if rippled by a warm breeze.

Standing in front of the bathroom mirror, Laurent gave up trying to shave. The electric razor, whose buzzing was the soundtrack to all his mornings, had made a tired groaning sound when he turned it on and had now stopped altogether, giving way to silence. He turned the razor off and on again, tapped the foil, unplugged it and plugged it back in again. Nothing. The Braun 860 with its three rotating blades had given up the ghost. Laurent was upset. He couldn't bear to throw the razor away, at least not yet. He laid it down reverentially in the clam dish brought back from Greece ten years ago. His Gillette razor that he found mouldering in a drawer also turned out to be useless, because of a second setback. When he turned on the bath tap, he was greeted by a dull hiss. No water. The notice announcing that the water would be turned off had been up in the hallway of his building for a week, but he'd forgotten. Laurent looked in the mirror and saw a badly shaven man with strangely dishevelled hair after a restless night. There was just enough water in the kettle for one cup of coffee.

As he left the building he glanced over at the metal shutter of the shop. Shortly he would raise it by turning a key in the electronic panel, then nod a greeting to his neighbour Jean Martel (of Le Temps Perdu, antiques – bric-a-brac – bought and sold) enjoying a café crème on the terrace of the Jean Bart. He would also wave to the lady from the dry-cleaner's (La Blanche Colombe – Specialist Dry-cleaning) who in turn would wave back through the window. Then after the shutter was up he would look over his own shop window as he always did with its 'New fiction', 'Art books', 'Bestsellers', alongside 'Books we love' and 'Must reads'.

On the stroke of ten-thirty, Maryse would arrive, followed by Damien. The team complete, the day could begin. They would unpack the deliveries of books and help customers with their varied requests. 'I'm looking for that novel about the Second World War. I can't remember who it's by or the name of the publisher.' And then there would be the recommendations. 'Madame Berthier, I really think you should try this. You were looking for something light to distract you. I guarantee you'll love it.' And the orders to put through. 'Yes, hello, Le Cahier Rouge here. Could I order three copies of *Don Juan*, Molière, the Bibliolycée paperback edition?' And the returns: 'Hello, it's Le Cahier Rouge. I'd like to return four copies of *Tristesse d'été*. It's not selling and I'm changing my displays.' There would be events to plan: 'Laurent Letellier from Le Cahier Rouge here. Would it be possible to organise a signing with your author …?'

When he had bought it, the bookshop had been a moribund café, Le Celtique, run by an elderly couple. They were waiting to sell up so that they could return to the Auvergne and Laurent was their unexpected saviour. The café had the added advantage of coming with a flat. That, however, was a mixed blessing. It eliminated travelling, but it also meant that Laurent never left his place of work.

Laurent walked round the square and up Rue de la Pentille. He was carrying the latest novel by Frédéric Pichier, who was coming in for a signing the following week. Laurent planned to reread the notes he had jotted in the book over a double espresso sitting outside l'Espérance café, where he often ended up on his morning perambulations. The book told the story of a young farm worker during the Great War. It was the fourth book from the author, who had made his name with *Tears of Sand*, the story of a Napoleonic soldier falling in love with a young Egyptian girl during the French campaign in the Middle East. Pichier was adept at setting the sufferings of his characters against the backdrop of great historical events. Laurent couldn't make up his mind whether Pichier was just a good storyteller or a real writer. There were arguments for both views. But in any case, the book was selling very well and the signing session would certainly be popular.

As he was walking along, Maryse sent him a text. Her train had been delayed and she might be late. 'Keep me posted, Maryse,' Laurent texted back before setting off along Rue Vivant-Denon. As he reached number 6, he checked to make sure his customer, Madame Merlier, had opened her blinds. The old lady, who looked remarkably like the actress Marguerite Moreno, was an avid reader and always rose early. She had remarked to Laurent one day, 'If I haven't opened my blinds, I'll either be dead or well on the way.' They had agreed that Laurent would call an ambulance if he ever saw the blinds down in daytime. But everything was fine at number 6; the blinds were open. Almost the only ones on the street in fact, apparently people were enjoying a lie-in. The area was deserted. He continued on his way down Rue du Passe-Musette. L'Espérance café was right at the end, on the corner between the boulevard and the weekend market. The bins had been put out in front of each courtyard door, some accompanied by pieces of old furniture awaiting the large waste collection. Laurent passed one of the bins, slowing down – it had taken a little time to register what he had seen – then turned back and retraced his steps.

There was a handbag on top of the bin. It was mauve leather and in very good condition. It had several compartments and zipped pockets, two broad handles, a shoulder strap and gold clasps. Instinctively Laurent glanced around him – an absurd thing to do; no woman was suddenly going to appear and come and claim her property. From the way the leather bulged it was obvious it wasn't empty. Had it been damaged and empty the owner would have thrown it into the bin, and not left it on top. In any case, did women ever throw their handbags away? Laurent thought about the woman who had shared his life for twelve years. No, Claire had never thrown away any of her bags. She had several and changed them with the seasons. She never threw away shoes either; not even when the little straps on her court shoes wore out – she would have them mended at the cobbler's. In fact, even when the shoes were beyond repair, Laurent had never seen a pair in the kitchen bin amongst the peelings. They just mysteriously disappeared. It was still possible that a woman *might* have thrown away her bag, despite these thoughts that took him back to his past. But on the other hand, the fact that the pristine bag was sitting on its own on top of the bin seemed to suggest something more sinister. A theft, for example.

Laurent lifted the bag. He half opened the main zip and saw that it did indeed contain many 'personal effects' as they were called. He was about to look through the bag when a young woman came out of a doorway, dragging a suitcase on wheels. She went past, then looked back at him. When her eye met Laurent's, she speeded up imperceptibly, then disappeared round the corner. At that moment, Laurent realised how shady he looked – a man on his own, ill-shaven with unkempt hair, opening a woman's handbag on top of a bin … He shut it hastily. What was the moral course of action now: to take it with him or to leave it where it was? Somewhere in the city, a woman had almost certainly been robbed of her bag and in all probability had given up hope of ever seeing it again. I'm the only one who knows where it is, he thought, and if I leave it here it will be destroyed by the refuse collectors or stolen all over again.

Laurent reached a decision: he picked it up and went off up the street. The police station was only ten minutes away. He would drop it off there, fill in a form or two, then come back and settle down in the café.

It was strange carrying the bag. Like walking a pet that had been given to you and which only followed you with great reluctance. Laurent held the gold strap like a lead, having wound it round his hand a bit so that the bag wouldn't swing about and attract attention. He was carrying something that wasn't his, that had no business being on his shoulder. Another woman had looked down at the bag then back up at Laurent.

As he made his way up the boulevard, his discomfort increased. He felt as if everyone he passed was covertly watching him, having instantly grasped what was wrong with the image: a man with a woman's bag. A mauve one. He would never have imagined that walking about with it would be such an uncomfortable experience. Yet he remembered how sometimes Claire had given him her bag while she went back up to the flat to get her cigarettes or went to the loo in a café. So he had found himself on the street holding a woman's handbag. He remembered that he had felt a sort of amused embarrassment but it had never lasted long. Claire would immediately reappear and reclaim her bag. On those rare occasions, Laurent saw that there were women who noticed that the bag belonged to a female, but he had never seen any suspicion in their glances, just amusement. He was obviously a man waiting for his wife. It was as evident as if he had been wearing a sandwich board reading 'My wife will be back shortly'.

A group of girls in jeans and Converse parted to let him pass and he heard a giggle followed by them all laughing. Were they laughing at him? He preferred not to know. Having attracted suspicion was he now a figure of fun? He crossed over and made his way to the police station through the back streets.

The waiting area had putty-coloured walls and a frosted-glass window with no handle. This space with its plastic chairs, Formica table and two offices with their doors wide open, where the public came to report the theft of personal belongings, seemed to be no more than a sort of limbo for missing handbags. Five women of various ages sat in silence. In one of the offices, an old woman with a walking stick and a plaster above her eye was sobbing as she recounted the theft of hers. The man with white hair who was with her didn't know where to look. Laurent found himself in one of those purgatorial places one hopes never to have to enter – accident and emergency, customs offices at airports, rehabilitation centres ... The kinds of places you pass thinking you are better off outside, even if it's raining.

'Anyway, our bags will never turn up,' said a small dark woman who was reading *Voici*.

A young sergeant appeared, carrying several photocopied sheets.

'Excuse me,' Laurent said to him. 'I've come to hand in a bag.'

The five waiting women looked up.

'You'll have to speak to one of my colleagues, Monsieur,' the sergeant replied hastily, indicating one of the offices.

A stocky man with a shaved head and little sunken eyes got up to show a woman out. He glanced at Laurent, who held out the mauve handbag.

'I've come to hand in a bag that I found in the street.'

'That's a fine act of citizenship,' replied the man. He spoke in a powerful voice, adding, 'Come and see this, Amélie.'

A plump little blonde woman came out of the same office and went over to them.

'I told this gentleman that he's performed a fine act of citizenship' – he seemed pleased with his expression – 'he's brought us a handbag.'

'I agree. Well done, Monsieur,' responded Amélie.

Laurent felt that the young policewoman approved of a man who would take the time to hand in a woman's bag.

'As you can see,' the powerful voice went on, this time with a hint of weariness, 'these ladies are waiting. I'll be with you in, let's say ...' looking at his watch, 'about an hour?'

'At least an hour,' corrected Amélie softly.

Her colleague nodded his agreement.

'Perhaps I'll come back tomorrow morning,' suggested Laurent.

'If you like – our offices are open from nine-thirty to one o'clock, and from two o'clock until seven,' the man said.

'Or you could go to the lost property office, Monsieur,' suggested the policewoman. 'It's at 36 Rue des Morillons, in the fifteenth.'

When he left the police station he found another text from Maryse: her train had only just started moving again – she would not be there by opening time. Laurent walked past l'Espérance without stopping; he would read his notes on Pichier at work.

The green dustcart had stopped in front of the apartments and two young refuse collectors plugged into iPods were hooking on the bins, which were then emptied noisily into the truck. There was no doubt that without Laurent, the bag would by now have been taken by someone or have ended up in landfill with only flies for company.

Laurent, the temporary guardian of someone else's belongings, went up to his apartment, put the bag on the sofa and went back down again to open the bookshop. The day could begin.

At twelve-thirty, having read the night porter's note about a slightly peculiar guest, the two reception staff began to worry. The woman should have left her room long before now, and by midday check-out at the latest. One of the men decided to go up with the master key. Having reached the room, he put his ear to the wooden door and listened for the shower. He couldn't go striding into a woman's room and risk catching her coming out of the bathroom naked; this had happened to him once before and he had no intention of making the same mistake again. But there was no sound coming from 52. He knocked several times but receiving no reply, he decided to go in.

'Reception, Madame,' he said, flicking the light switch. 'Since you haven't vacated your room, I took the liberty of—'

He stopped in his tracks. Laure was sprawled on the bed, her half-naked body lying between the cover and the sheet. With her eyes closed, she appeared to be asleep. He took a step forward. Her head was resting on the pillow.

'Mademoiselle,' he said loudly, and again, 'Mademoiselle,' as he edged towards the bed. He was becoming more and more certain that something was not right. 'What the hell's going on?' he muttered. He said the word 'Mademoiselle' once more, knowing it would be met with silence.

He leant in closer. Her face was perfectly still, the features regular and relaxed. In spite of his growing concern, he found himself noticing she was pretty before forcing himself to focus on establishing one key point: was she breathing? He thought so. He reached over and touched her shoulder. No reaction. He shook her gently. 'Mademoiselle ...' Her eyes remained shut and she did not stir. The hotel employee stared hard at the woman's bare breasts, watching to see if the chest rose and fell. Yes, all was well, she was breathing. A pigeon landed noisily on the balcony, making him jump. Without thinking, he swiftly pulled back the curtains, sunlight flooded the room and the bird flew off. Perched on a chair in the window of the building opposite was a black cat whose dilated eyes seemed to stare back at him. The man lifted the phone beside the bed and dialled nine for reception.

'Julien,' he said. 'There's a problem with the guest in 52 ...'

As he spoke, his gaze fell on the pillow. Under Laure's head, there was a large patch of dried blood and her hair was stuck to the towel beneath it.

'A big problem,' he corrected himself. 'Call an ambulance, immediately.'

Half an hour later, Laure was wheeled out on a folding stretcher, pushed thirty metres along the pavement and lifted into the back of the red vehicle. The words 'haematoma', 'head injury' and 'coma' were mentioned.

In the boiling-hot shower, shampoo ran down his face. Laurent had sold twenty-eight novels, nine coffee-table books, seven children's books, five graphic novels, four essays, and three guides to Paris and France. He had filled in four loyalty cards and placed fourteen orders. Then the day had finally come to an end and he had been able to close the shop and come up to his flat, noticing on the way that the water was back on. He had spent all day apologising with a smile for his dishevelled appearance. One of his customers had said he looked like Chateaubriand, another like Rimbaud in Fantin-Latour's painting *Un coin de table* (whilst making it clear that he was only referring to the poet's hair).

Laurent dried his face then took the razor from the drawer and an old can of Williams shaving foam he had luckily kept. Close-shaven, he put on clean jeans, a white shirt and loafers and brushed his hair back, preparing for the opening of the bag as if he were going out to dinner with a woman.

In his inbox he found all sorts of spam. Mostly offering him, in the warmest first-name terms, insurance or a holiday to an exorbitantly expensive destination – but all at half price! 'Leave today,' announced one. Another suggested in that chummy digital way, 'Laurent, time for a holiday.' He was also exhorted to buy one of those oddities you come across on the internet, in this case an umbrella for dogs. The email urged him in all seriousness to hurry to acquire this indispensable accessory – 'Your loyal companion will be so grateful.' In the midst of this digital forest there was not a single personal message. Yet he was due to have dinner soon with his daughter. No doubt she would appear in his inbox shortly – Chloé never forgot an arrangement.

He took the remains of the *hachis Parmentier* from the fridge and decided to open a bottle of Fixin from the case one of his loyal clients had given him. He tasted it; the Burgundy was perfect. Glass in hand, he went back to the sitting room.

The bag was there, on the sofa. He was about to open it when he received a text. Dominique: 'Maybe see you this evening, but very late, complicated day, will explain later, still at the office. The Bourse is crashing, if you watch the news you'll see how I'm spending my evening! xxx'. Laurent drank some wine then sent back a sober 'Let me know xxx'. Then he sat down crosslegged on the floor, with his glass beside him and picked up the bag carefully. It was beautiful. Mauve leather, gold clasps and external pockets of various sizes. There was nothing comparable for men. They had to make do with satchels, or otherwise briefcases which were all a standard shape intended only for carrying paperwork. He drank some more wine, feeling he was about to commit a forbidden act. A transgression. For a man should never go through a woman's handbag – even the most remote tribe would adhere to that ancestral rule. Husbands in loincloths definitely did not have the right to go and look for a poisoned arrow or a root to eat in their wives' rawhide bags.

Laurent had never opened a woman's handbag. He hadn't opened his mother's when he was a child and he hadn't opened Claire's either. Occasionally he had been told, 'Take the keys from my bag,' or 'There's a pack of tissues in my bag; you can take those.' He had not touched a handbag without explicit prior authorisation, more like a command that was only valid for a very limited time. If Laurent couldn't find the keys or the tissues in less than ten seconds and began to rummage about in the bag, it was immediately reclaimed by its owner. The action was accompanied by an irritated little exclamation, always in the imperative, 'Give that to me!' And the keys or tissues would magically appear.

He gently pulled the zip open all the way. The bag gave off an odour of warm leather and women's perfume.

What I really need is a friend just like me; I'm sure I'd be my own best friend.

Last night's dream: Belphégor was a man, which was a bit of a surprise, but in a way it wasn't. I knew it was him — he made quite an attractive man. We were going back up to our room in a luxury hotel after a drink at the bar. We were falling asleep on the bed and then making love on the terrace (it was good). I woke up and he was rubbing his nose against mine (that bit was real, not in the dream). BUY CAT FOOD, Virbac <u>duck flavour</u>.

I like:
Walking along the water's edge just as everyone else is leaving the beach.
The name 'americano', but I prefer to drink a 'mojito'.
The smell of mint, and basil.
Sleeping on trains.
Paintings of landscapes without people.
The smell of incense in churches.
Velvet and panne velvet.
Having lunch in the garden.
Erik Satie. Buy an ERIK SATIE BOX SET.

I'm scared of birds (especially pigeons).
Think of other things 'I'm scared of'.

On my way home, I always scan the Métro carriage for 'possible'
men. (I've never met a man on the Métro.)
I need to break up with Hervé. Hervé is boring. There's nothing
worse than being bored with a boring man.
I like open fires. I like the smell of burning wood. The smell of a
wood fire.
I've broken up with Hervé. I don't like breaking up. Think of other
things 'I don't like'.

It was almost eleven o'clock. Still sitting on the floor but now
surrounded by objects, Laurent was absorbed in the red Moleskine
notebook. The thoughts of the unknown woman were written
over several pages, sometimes with crossings out, underlinings,
or words written in capital letters. The handwriting was elegant
and fluid. She must have recorded her thoughts in the notebook
as the whim took her, on café terraces or on the Métro. Laurent
was fascinated by her reflections which followed on one from the
other, random, touching, zany, sensual. He had opened a door
into the soul of the woman with the mauve bag and even though
he felt what he was doing was inappropriate, he couldn't stop
himself from reading on. A quote from Sacha Guitry came to
mind: 'Watching someone sleep is like reading a letter that's not
addressed to you.' The bottle of wine was half empty and the
hachis Parmentier forgotten on the kitchen counter.

The first thing he had found was a black glass bottle of perfume
– Habanita by Molinard. He pressed once on the spray, releasing
the powdery scent of ylang-ylang and jasmine. Then came a
bunch of keys on a decorative key ring with a gilt cartouche

covered in hieroglyphics. Next a little diary with appointment times circled on the appropriate day, with first names, sometimes full names noted. No addresses or telephone numbers. For this month, January, it was filled halfway through. Laurent recognised the make of diary; Le Cahier Rouge sold similar ones in their stationery section. Its owner had not bothered to write her own details on the page at the front that was intended for that purpose. The last event listed was for the previous evening: 8 p.m., dinner Jacques and Sophie + Virginie. No address for that entry either. Just one entry for the coming week, on Thursday: 6 p.m., dry-cleaner's (strappy dress). Next he took out a little fawn and violet leather bag containing make-up and accessories, including a large brush whose softness he tested against his cheek. A gold lighter, a black Montblanc ballpoint (perhaps the one used to jot down her thoughts in the notebook), a packet of liquorice sweets – he took one and it immediately added an interesting woody flavour to the taste of the Fixin – a small bottle of Evian, a hair clip with a blue flower on it, and a pair of red plastic dice. Laurent picked them up and rolled them on the floor. Five and six. Good throw. A recipe for *ris de veau* torn from a women's magazine, *Elle* probably. A packet of tissues. A telephone charger, but of course, no phone or wallet. And nothing with her name or address on it.

There were four colour photographs in a folded envelope. One of a middle-aged man with grey-white hair, dressed in a red polo shirt and beige trousers. He was standing against a backdrop of pine trees, smiling. Next to him, a woman of similar age in a lilac dress, blonde with dark glasses, held her hand out to the person taking the photograph. It looked as if it had been taken more than twenty years ago, thirty maybe. The next photo showed a much younger man with short brown hair standing with his arms crossed in front of an apple tree. In the third one there was a house and garden with a large tree. There was nothing to indicate the location of the house and none of the photographs were annotated. Here were memories and loved ones that revealed nothing and which only the owner of the handbag would be able to identify.

There seemed to be no end to the items in the bag. Laurent decided to take several out at once. He thrust his hand into the left side pocket and pulled out a jumble of things. A copy of *Pariscope*, lip balm, Nurofen, a hairgrip and a book. *Accident Nocturne* by Patrick Modiano. Laurent paused for a moment. So the bag's owner read Modiano, a novelist whose favourite themes were mystery, memory and the search for identity. It was as if Modiano was sending him a message. When had he written that book? Laurent couldn't quite remember, but he thought it was around 2000. He opened the book to find the year it was originally published. 'Gallimard 2003' was printed at the bottom of the left-hand page and there was something else visible on the other side of the page. Some handwriting showed through. Laurent turned the page back and read the two lines written in pen beneath the title: 'For Laure, in memory of our meeting in the rain. Patrick Modiano.' The writing blurred before his eyes. Modiano, the most elusive of French authors. Who hadn't done any book signings for years and only rarely gave interviews. Whose hesitant diction, full of pauses, had become legendary and who was himself a legend. An enigma that his readers had followed from book to book for forty years. To have a book signed by him seemed highly improbable. And yet here was his signature in black and white.

The author of *Rue des Boutiques Obscures* had just provided him with the first name of the woman with the mauve bag.

I'm scared of red ants.

And of logging on to my bank account and clicking 'current balance'.

I'm scared when the telephone rings first thing in the morning.

And of getting on the Métro when it's packed.

I'm scared of time passing.

I'm scared of electric fans, but I know why.

It was time to stop reading Laure's red notebook and get on with emptying the bag to look for any clue, however tiny, that might provide him with the owner's name or address. He still had more pockets to look in, some zipped and some not. Laurent would never have imagined that a woman's bag could have so many nooks and crannies. It was even more complicated than dissecting an octopus on a kitchen table. Several times he thought he had emptied a pocket only to find a lump at the bottom which turned out to be a stone, no doubt picked up at some meaningful moment. He had found three of them in all, in different parts of the bag. And a conker, probably picked up in a park.

He paused in his task, and got up to open the window, letting in the cold night air. The square was deserted. His head was spinning – was it because of the wine and lack of dinner or because of the accumulation of objects he had unearthed? He wasn't really sure. Laurent was about to go back to his inventory when his phone beeped. He had completely forgotten about Dominique. Her text read, 'Be with you in five minutes, hope you haven't gone to bed yet.' He had not finished with the bag but immediately began to put everything back inside, not without feeling a certain resentment towards Dominique who was forcing him to interrupt his investigation just as it was beginning. Then he shoved the bag regretfully into his wardrobe.

As he combed his hair in front of the mirror, he reflected that he could easily have left all the items on the floor and explained the story to Dominique. But he hadn't wanted to. Dominique would have been jealous and suspicious, and Laurent did not want to share his discovery. For the moment, Modiano's Laure was a mystery he would keep to himself.

'You've had a woman here ...'

'I beg your pardon?' replied Laurent.

Dominique's dark eyes bored into his, and her short haircut, which suited her fine features so well, now seemed to make her look like a bird of prey.

'There's been no woman here,' said Laurent with as much assurance as he could muster at that hour. How on earth could Dominique divine the presence of a woman's belongings in the room twenty minutes earlier? It was commonly said that women had a sixth sense. But this was surely a case of witchcraft.

Dominique twisted her wine glass in her hand and tapped her cigarette ash into the crystal ashtray.

'A woman has been here – I can smell her perfume,' she said with a knowing look.

The black bottle in the bag. It had been a bad idea to try out the spray; the smell of Habanita must still be in the air. Yet it had only been one quick spray and more than two hours had passed.

Like a bloodhound Dominique had picked up the scent in a way that Laurent was certain no other woman could have done.

'There have been no women here. I swear to you ... on my daughter's life, on my bookshop, that if a woman has been in this room, I will be ruined in a matter of months.'

Laurent had chosen his words carefully. He could swear on anything he liked because he had spoken the truth: no woman had been in his apartment. It was only her bag that had taken up residence.

The speech appeared to pacify Dominique. 'I believe you,' she said. 'You're too superstitious to lie about something like that.' She then went on to tell him how she had had to spend her evening watching screens recording the latest tumbles of stock markets around the world and the final million-dollar transactions, in order to write her column for the famous newspaper where she was economics editor. Dominique also had a radio slot and sometimes appeared on television for TF1. It was always strange to see the woman he shared his nights with on the small screen chatting with other journalists and sometimes even with big names in broadcasting.

They had met when Laurent had been invited on to TF1 to talk about a high-profile book and Dominique had been waiting to go on to do her economics broadcast. She had read the book he had talked about and told him how much she liked it. The author was doing a signing the following week at Le Cahier Rouge and Laurent had invited her along. She was still there at closing time. Their eyes had met for that fraction of a second during which, without saying a word, a man and a woman who don't know each other signal that the night is not yet over.

'Well, anyway, it's late,' she said, leading the way to the bedroom.

As he embraced her on the bed, Laurent could not help turning his head towards the wardrobe where he had hidden the bag, and, as Dominique kissed him, the phrase 'I'm scared of red ants' seemed to take root permanently in his brain.

Laurent turned over in bed and realised he was alone. He looked at the clock: it was six in the morning. Even when Dominique got up early, she never left before seven, and not without saying goodbye. Laurent got up and found her fully dressed in the hall, about to leave.

'You're going?'

'That's right. I'm leaving.'

'Why are you looking at me like that?'

'I've left you a note on the coffee table,' Dominique replied coldly, doing up the belt on her coat.

> *Laurent,*
>
> *As you were so keen to swear on them, I would keep an eye on your daughter and the finances of your bookshop. I got up early this morning and went to lie down for a moment on the sofa. This is what I found on your carpet. Perhaps we can discuss it one day. Or perhaps not. That's up to you. I won't be the one making the first move, I can assure you.*
>
> *Dominique*

Under her signature, Dominique had conspicuously placed the hairgrip from the bag. Laurent must have dropped it as he was hurriedly putting everything back in the bag.

'You're not going to tell me it's your daughter's.'

'No, it's not my daughter's. I can explain, if you wait a moment.' He fetched the bag from his wardrobe and set it on the coffee table.

'It just gets better,' murmured Dominique, amazed by Laurent's brazen gesture. 'She actually leaves her things here.'

'No, it's not that at all! You'll laugh when I tell you the truth.'

'Go on then, Laurent, make me laugh.'

'I found the bag in the street.'

'You must think I'm an idiot.' Dominique's face was suddenly impassive and Laurent experienced the vertigo of the falsely accused who finds that absolutely no one believes him, not even his own lawyer.

'No,' stammered Laurent, 'I don't think you're an idiot. I found it yesterday in the street. In Rue du Passe-Musette to be precise.'

Dominique nodded slowly, but her expression was getting colder and colder.

'A full bag, in the street ...'

'Yes, a stolen bag; it had been stolen,' replied Laurent.

'And what was it doing in your cupboard, this stolen bag?'

Laurent opened his mouth to reply but he didn't get the chance.

'Why didn't you tell me this fanciful tale last night?'

'Well, because—'

'Because I wasn't supposed to find the hairgrip on the carpet!' Dominique cut him off heatedly.

Laurent was speechless.

'The first thing I could smell here was her perfume,' went on Dominique, walking unseeingly round the room. 'I should have suspected something, you were being weird ...'

'It wasn't her perfume. Well, yes, it was, but it was me who sprayed it,' he said, rummaging around in the bag. 'Where's the bottle got to? I'll show you; it's here somewhere. Why can you never find anything in a handbag?' Laurent was getting annoyed. 'Here it is,' he exclaimed triumphantly. He pressed the nozzle and a light spray fanned out in the morning light.

'I'm impressed,' commented Dominique soberly. 'You can tell her that I don't like her perfume.'

Laurent heard the door slam. He was left standing stock still in the middle of the sitting room, the black bottle of Habanita in his hand.

He hastily pulled on his clothes so that he could run after her, but Dominique had already found a taxi, which was disappearing round a corner of the square. Her phone went straight to voicemail. Laurent didn't bother to leave a message. Instead he sank down onto a stool at the counter of the Jean-Bart, where Jean Martel had just returned from some early morning antique hunting. The antique dealer had laid out several snuff boxes and was examining them with a pocket magnifying glass.

'It's like an investigation,' said the old trader; 'you have to choose a clue and see where it leads.'

'And what is the clue?' Laurent asked him wearily.

'There's a partially erased coat of arms on this one – I think it's a count's. If I can identify him, perhaps I can find out where it came from.'

Laurent nodded, paid for his coffee then went back up to his flat. The bag was on the table beside the note. *Perhaps we can discuss it one day. Or perhaps not. That's up to you.* He would call her later in the day. It was very unfair – it certainly looked as if he had done something wrong, but he had the right to defend himself, to explain properly. Although that was what he had done and Dominique hadn't believed him.

After another cup of coffee, he looked at his emails. More spam including the dog umbrellas – they were certainly persistent.

From: kloestar@gmail.com
To: laurent_letellier@hotmail.com
Subject: Meeting with ME!

Hey Brainy Bookwhizz
Are we still on for Monday evening? Meet me at Chez François at exactly six o'clock. It's that café with the tables outside near the lycée, up on the left in front of the big tree and the statue, the one we had lunch at last month. Get a table facing the street. Right at the front. Wear your black jacket and white shirt with those blue 501s we bought together last Saturday. Then we can have dinner. What are you going to cook? I'd like one of your pot-au-feus.

C. xxx

Laurent smiled. The message sounded like an imperious summons from his mistress. But it was nothing of the sort — just a message from his fifteen-year-old daughter. Feisty, very pretty and, according to her mother, 'appallingly manipulative', Chloé had taken her parents' separation in her stride. 'I think it's perfectly reasonable,' she had told her father from the great height of her twelve years, 'but I don't want to lose out.'

'I'm sorry? I'm not sure I understand.'

'I want double pocket money.'

'I'm sorry?' said Laurent again.

'As I'm going to live with Maman, I'd like a cat.'

That time Laurent had not said 'I'm sorry' again. Instead he had sat down on the velour sofa and taken a long look at this scrap of womanhood, a blend apparently of his and Claire's genes. There must have been some kind of mutation. As a child he would never have had that much nerve, and neither would Claire.

'There's a white female kitten for sale in the next-door apartment block,' Claire had told her a few weeks later.

'I don't want a white female kitten, I want a male. A big one. A Maine Coon.'

Claire had told Laurent about this demand, referring frequently to 'your daughter'.

Now Chloé lived with her mother and an enormous Maine Coon.

'What are you going to call it, darling?' Claire and Laurent had asked her.

'Putin,' Chloé had replied slowly, smiling for added effect.

'No!' cried Claire. 'You can't call your cat Putin.' But her words made no difference.

Putin never left Chloé's room except to go to his food bowl or litter tray. He refused to let anyone other than Chloé stroke him, and would stride disdainfully across the living room to sharpen his claws on the sofa under the horrified eye of Claire, before going back to his room to await the return of his mistress.

Laurent typed back:

All right, my love. I'll be there. And I'll make pot-au-feu. But less of the 'brainy bookwhizz'.

Lots of love

The moment he'd sent it, he reflected that he had probably never actually said 'no' to her. He took out his folding card table from behind the bookcase and resumed the task he had abandoned the night before. He put the bag on the green baize and took all the items out, laying them down at random. There was a tiny pocket in the lining where he found two unused Métro tickets and a dry-cleaning chit. Thursday's date was ticked, and the word 'dress' encircled. He checked the diary. It was obviously the ticket for the strappy dress, but it was just a generic ticket with no logo or address.

What was she like, this Laure who enjoyed having lunch in the garden, was frightened of red ants, dreamt she was making love to her pet which had been transformed into a man, and had a signed Patrick Modiano?

She was an enigma. It was like looking at someone through a fogged-up window. Her face was like one encountered in a dream, whose features dissolve as soon as you try to recall them.

'She's probably some old slag.'

The sentence had dropped like a fly into a bowl of milk, and Laurent rolled his eyes. He was lunching at the Jean-Bart with his friend Pascal Masselou, considered his 'best friend' since adolescence. The years had rolled by. Did Pascal still merit the appellation? He certainly didn't have any competition for the title. But in fact the two men had little in common now. Their family situation was the same though; they were both divorced. But apart from that, everything that had bound them together had been left behind in the past. Messing about together in class, fantasising about supposedly inaccessible girls, giggling and shared secrets, beers in the bar, then university degrees all seemed light years away from the adults they had become. They had kept their relationship going like two poker players who continue late into the night, shuffling their cards and emptying their glasses long after the others have left the table and gone to bed. Laurent had told him about the bag, wanting to believe for a moment that Pascal would share his fascination.

'Why do you say that?'

'Because you don't know who she is and you never will,' replied Pascal, chewing his entrecôte. 'All you have is the bag and her first name, no address and, most importantly, no photos. When I go after a woman, I know who she is, everything about her: what she looks like, how old she is, what we have in common, what she does, the colour of her eyes and hair, height, weight ...'

Since his divorce Pascal had discovered dating sites on the web. Usually he signed up to them under various pseudonyms. He was spreading himself about in the cyber jungle of the lonely hearts ads and had several times tried to convince Laurent to join him. He used 'SeniorExec' on Meetic and Attractive World – and the more evocative, not to say grotesque, 'Shivers', 'Jimmy', 'Magnum' and 'TheBest' on respectively: Adultery.com, Infidelity.fr, AshleyMadison.com, Adopt-a-bloke.com. Available for no-strings intimacy evenings and weekends, he was also in the market for 'serious' relationships, thereby easing his conscience.

'I'm making the most of it,' he liked to say, with a satisfied smile.

It seemed to Laurent that Pascal had been seduced by the very worst that the Western world offered, managing his love life, or, not to put too fine a point on it, his sex life, like the product manager of a small business. At a previous lunch, he had shown Laurent the relevant files on his laptop. In one click, Pascal had made three folders appear, filled with photos of women. 'Stock' for the women he had already slept with, 'In progress' for those he'd had a date with, 'Prospective' for the women he was aiming to date soon.

'Seriously? You haven't really made folders ...'

'Of course I have,' Pascal said, irritated. 'And within each folder I've put them into categories: nymphomaniacs, shy, teases, frigid ...'

'For goodness' sake, don't show me that,' Laurent had protested.

Pascal had shrugged and closed his laptop. He considered Laurent hopelessly old-fashioned, still believing in the chance encounter, the smile exchanged across a café terrace, or the conversation about a book that led on to something else. Laurent, on the other hand, considered that Pascal had become his own pimp, posting photos of himself worthy of a *GQ* fashion shoot: smiling, face on, a full-length shot, shirt open, grey jacket slung over one shoulder; or else bare-chested in swimming trunks in a shot taken five years ago on a Corsican beach. He had ticked the answers to questions like 'What would you say are your best qualities?' or 'What sort of relationship are you looking for – a: serious, b: just friends, c: open?'

Now Pascal was updating Laurent on how his life was going. His son had had a scooter accident, and his daughter wasn't speaking to him, ever since her friend's older sister had shown her a photo of the guy she was flirting with on the net and it turned out to be … Pascal. Laurent had decided not to take Pascal up to his flat to show him the bag. Before the lunch, that had been his intention but obviously it would be a mistake. He didn't want Pascal looking over all the items from the bag, and he wanted even less to hear his rude comments: women's nonsense, you're wasting your time, why don't you throw it all in the bin? You want to meet someone? Create a profile on one of the sites.

'And how's Dominique?'

'Yes, she's very well, thank you,' replied Laurent quietly.

'I heard her this morning on the radio; her analysis was spot on! She's an intelligent, good-looking woman – you're lucky to have her.' And as he finished up his béarnaise, Pascal concluded, 'You're made for each other.'

Laurent did not react. He had to admit that his friend was right. Without an identity card, or any photos, the woman with the red notebook would remain a mystery, and in all probability her things would soon be consigned to lost property.

A garden. Very much like the one of her childhood home. Only, not quite the same. In this one, there was a sort of rockery right at the bottom by the little brick wall. If she concentrated, she could even hear the water running over the stones. She had the distinct impression that a fat Siamese cat was sleeping in the sun on her bare feet. Even though it seemed unlikely, she was certain of it: she was in the garden. The feeling of the grass against her skin was so real. The cat sleeping at her feet that she couldn't see could only be Sarbacane.

Her parents were there too. Somewhere near the table under the big tree where they ate lunch in summer. Her father would go to the market in the square and bring back oysters and spider crabs. He would open the oysters himself while her mother cooked the crabs in a court bouillon with bay leaves. Their shells went bright red. And when you squeezed lemon juice over the membrane of an oyster, it shrank back. That shows it's fresh, her father used to say.

It was almost time for lunch, at some point in the early eighties, and the clocks had stopped ticking then. The last thirty years had fallen away. Laure had only dreamt she had become an adolescent and then a grown-up, that she had a job and a flat and service charges to pay. The very idea of a little girl paying service charges! At that age, the only problems you should be tackling were sums and spellings: past participles with *avoir* agree with the direct object when it comes before the verb. Why, though? Because they do. Yes, but why? Honestly, don't ask stupid questions, that's just the way it is, full stop; you just have to learn it; we've had enough of your questions, Laure.

She had dreamt every encounter, every winding road that had led her to the silence of the Ateliers Gardhier. She had dreamt she would one day meet Xavier Valadier. I'm a photo-journalist, I take pictures in war zones. That must be very dangerous ... Yes, it can be, he smiled. That gentle, sad smile and the two dimples that appeared with it had enchanted her. Just like his eyes, which must have seen too much death around the world. She had dreamt too his portfolio with its pictures of veiled Afghan women, children in the rubble of Chechnya, Hezbollah militants in Lebanon. And the one of Xavier posing beside Ahmed Shah Massoud. That name: Ahmed Shah Massoud, pronounced in an Arabic accent with the tongue rolling against the incisors. The whole thing was just a dream.

Just as it was five years later, when the telephone rang in the apartment at twenty past seven in the morning and the voice of a woman from the foreign ministry came down the line. That embarrassed, hesitant voice with a note of fear in it. The tone of voice that told Laure that her life was about to collapse. Like those ice sheets weighing several tons which break off icebergs with the first thaw and slide into the frozen waters of the Antarctic. The voice said: Something has happened to your husband in Iraq, something serious, very serious ... There was a long silence before Laure asked, Is he dead ... Is that what you're saying? Then a shorter silence before the two words, Yes, Madame, were spoken.

Xavier was there in the garden too; she was sure she could

47

hear his voice over by the tree. He was talking to her father. Her mother was in the kitchen and Sarbacane would be weaving between her legs trying to pick up stray bits of crab. Everything about this summer afternoon was so real, and yet the house had long since been sold and everyone was dead. Sarbacane the cat was buried at the bottom of the garden by the brick wall, in the same spot as the strange water feature which had never existed. Laure's parents were in Montparnasse cemetery and Xavier's ashes had been scattered very early one blustery morning at Cap de la Hague.

The sounds she could hear suddenly bore no relation to those of the garden. Two female voices were exchanging opinions on the latest episodes of an American TV series. They were fully agreed on the lead actor's charms. One of them kept raving about his silver hair and commanding voice. That's what I call a real man! she exclaimed. No, it was definitely not the early eighties any more. The voices came closer. Baulieu says she should come out of it soon. Has any family been in to see her? A tall, skinny boy with short dyed-blond hair turned up last night in a complete flap, replied the other voice. He was a bit camp – well, more than a bit. He stayed until the end of visiting hours, said she's his sister, but they don't have the same surname.

William, Laure wanted to say. That was William. But no sound came out of her mouth. Nothing. And without meaning to, she headed back to the garden. The spider crabs were ready and her mother was calling her to fetch the white wine. She got up off the grass and went into the kitchen. She felt the cold floor tiles under her bare feet and when she opened the fridge, she saw her father had set two bottles of Pouilly-Fuissé to chill.

At this time of year there weren't many people sitting outside the café. Laurent chose a table right at the front, that's to say, just set back from the pavement. He settled down under one of the gas heaters which were dotted around the terrace to keep customers warm. Black jacket, white shirt, Levi's and a blue scarf Claire had given him ten years ago; everything exactly as Chloé had asked. It was almost six o'clock. He ordered an espresso and passed the time studying the people around him. There was a group of men who had left work early and were sipping beers. They looked tired but were forcing themselves to laugh as they exchanged work anecdotes. And there was a woman on her own, a few tables away, apparently absorbed in her e-reader. Laurent tilted his chair imperceptibly and leant towards her. With this device an entire library could be downloaded and carried about in a handbag. Would the printed book hold out against that marvel of technology? In spite of the success of Le Cahier Rouge, Laurent somehow doubted it.

Black bag over her shoulder, faded jeans, studded belt, high-heeled light suede ankle boots – a source of discord with her mother – her favourite sky-blue jacket, and a polo neck, black this time, Chloé was in her habitual outfit that nevertheless took her half an hour to choose each morning, according to Claire. She was slightly ahead of her friends who were standing at the end of the street, in front of the lycée, the oldest of them smoking. She came over to the table, dumped her bag down, and sat. 'So, Mr Bookseller, sold many books?'

'Aren't you going to give me a kiss?'

'Yes, but later,' she said, turning towards the end of the street. 'I'm so tired. I've had such a long day – you've no idea. It was horrible.'

'You're right, I've no idea,' murmured Laurent.

'And I'm thirsty,' she went on. 'Exhausted and completely dehydrated. I'd like a shandy.'

'Absolutely not, no alcohol outside the house.'

'Lemonade?'

'OK.'

'What would Mademoiselle like?' asked the waiter.

'Fresh lemonade, two ice cubes, a slice of lemon and a straw.'

'Certainly, Mademoiselle,' replied the waiter, exchanging a look with Laurent.

Chloé glanced quickly down the street, then turned back to her father.

'Are you waiting for someone?'

'No, no, why do you ask?' She was immediately defensive.

'No reason ... I made a pot-au-feu.'

'Great! I love your pot-au-feu. Bertand often makes it in winter, and he always ruins it, he's such a dick.'

'Please don't talk like that.'

Chloé said nothing and turned towards the lycée again. Bertrand was the new man in Claire's life. He was a photographer but only took photos of food. His clients ranged from the best delicatessens to the frozen food industry. Bertrand had no doubt dreamt of becoming the next Richard Avedon or Guy Bourdin, of having celebrities and models in front of his lens; but he had to make do instead with roast beef and forest chanterelle mushrooms or maybe fillet of hake with beurre blanc. But he had set up his own company employing six people, and he earned a good living, having cornered the market in high-end food photography. He never read a book, either fiction or non-fiction; all he read were articles on photography or food.

Laurent looked at his daughter: at the discreet make-up on her impeccable profile, the bridge of her nose – pronounced without being too dominant – almond-shaped eyes, delicately drawn brows and shapely mouth. She had become a very pretty young woman. And she had Claire's hands, long and slender, with wrists so small that most watchstraps had to have extra holes put in them. 'You've got new bracelets?' remarked Laurent.

'You noticed? They're so pretty, they're from this really cool new website. I'm so happy with them.'

Two blonde girls with long hair, in miniskirts and Converse, backpacks over their shoulders, were walking up towards the café. The waiter ceremoniously presented the glass of lemonade with two ice cubes, a slice of lemon on the rim and a pink straw.

'Fab,' said Chloé, pulling her chair closer to her father. 'Lovely to be here, together,' she said, snuggling up to him ostentatiously.

'I'm always very happy to be with you; I'm proud of you too,' said Laurent, smiling.

The two girls stopped right beside their table. Chloé looked up at them. The girls gazed silently at her then turned to Laurent.

The girl with the shorter hair asked in an arrogant little voice, 'You're Chloé's dad, aren't you?'

At that moment, under the table, the pointed heel of a suede boot landed on Laurent's right foot. He froze, then felt a sudden pang. He turned to look at his daughter. He knew her too well not to grasp what the eyes fixed on his face were expressing: panic and pleading. 'Yes, I'm her father. And to whom do I have the honour of speaking?' was obviously not the desired response. In the fraction of a second he still had to answer, and as the heel was refusing to relinquish the pressure, Laurent had time to tell himself that surely his daughter would not dare ... And yet a little voice inside him replied: Yes, she would, Laurent. You know your daughter; that's exactly what she would do. What else could this mean?

So he turned slowly to the girls and, smiling coldly, replied, 'Why do you ask that, Mesdemoiselles?'

'Well, uh ... because ...' stuttered the girl with the longer blonde hair.

'He's not my dad, he's my boyfriend,' announced Chloé proudly. 'Perhaps we could be left on our own now?' she went on, pretending to be irritated, and withdrawing her boot from her father's shoe. The two girls both took a step back, without taking their eyes off Laurent.

'Very sorry,' murmured the longer-haired girl.

'Sorry,' added the other, who had turned pale, 'we're leaving.'

Then they hurried across the road, side by side. Laurent watched them walking away on the opposite pavement. They were talking agitatedly and then one pushed the other in rage. 'I've never been more embarrassed in my life,' she screeched up at the darkening sky.

'They'll be slashing their wrists tonight,' Chloé said sardonically.

Passing her father off as her boyfriend! Chloé had gone too far. But as they drove home, all Laurent's arguments were rebuffed one by one by Chloé: he had no idea; in *Laurent's* day everything had been *different*. Laurent's ideas were prehistoric; back in his day there were no mobile phones and you had to be rung up on your parents' phone; boys were terrified of pretty girls and the worst they ever did was get hold of *Playboy* and goggle at the double-page spreads of naked women in suspenders in sexy poses. It was nothing like that now. To listen to his daughter was to imagine that, apart from her best friend Charlène, her school was entirely populated by narcissistic bitches, who only ever talked about painting their nails. As for the boys, they were just a bunch of psychopaths who spent their entire time watching hardcore porn on the internet and then offering to practise what they'd watched on Chloé. But the scene in the café had rendered Chloé 'untouchable'; no one would dare proposition her now; she would be left in peace. The news, now verified, that she had a handsome, much older boyfriend would be all over the lycée in seconds – in fact, it was probably already on Facebook.

Yes, people had asked her who he was, on the few occasions he had come to collect her from school. Yes, one day she had said he was not her father; yes, she had asked him to sit in that exact spot in the café on purpose so that those bitches would see her with him. No, she hadn't thought they would actually dare speak to them. And thank you for going along with it, you're awesome.

'Awesome,' grumbled Laurent.

Then when he heard, 'Anyway, you should be super flattered,' he was torn between slapping her and forgiving her. In the interests of a pleasant evening, he opted for the latter.

'What on earth is all this?'

Laurent had gone into the kitchen to heat up the pot-au-feu and Chloé was at the card table.

'The contents of a handbag,' said Laurent from the kitchen, before joining Chloé in the sitting room. 'I found it in the street.'

'I'd love to have that lipstick, but Maman won't buy it for me,' murmured Chloé. 'And that mirror, so pretty!'

'It was stolen. There's no ID, just the personal items – they're all there.'

Chloé was running her hands over everything, touching the keys, the dice, the *Pariscope*, the heap of stones. She opened the red notebook at random.

More things I like:

Summer evenings when it gets dark late.

Opening my eyes underwater.

The names 'Trans-Siberian Express' and 'Orient Express' (I'll never travel on either).

Lapsang Souchong tea.

Haribo Fraises Tagada.

Watching men sleep after making love.

Hearing 'Mind the gap' on the Tube in London.

'I'd like to find her,' Laurent announced. 'And the only clue I have is that,' he said, indicating the dry-cleaning ticket. Laurent had thought quite a lot about the issue of the dress. He had come to the conclusion that he would have to visit all the dry-cleaners' within a radius of about a kilometre. His thinking was as follows: Laure had had her bag stolen; the man had run off with it, then, once he was a few streets away, he'd rummaged in it, removing the purse, the bank card and the ID, which could be sold. He'd also grabbed the mobile phone, and perhaps one or two other items of value, and then abandoned the bag on top of the bin, before making off. Laurent had found the bag in the morning, so the theft must either have happened shortly before, or in the night. If that analysis was correct, there were then two possibilities. Either Laure had been passing through the area, or she lived there. She would presumably have gone to a dry-cleaner's relatively near her home, perhaps a dry-cleaner who knew her name. So if she lived in the area, the dry-cleaner's would be nearby.

'Look at the things, Chloé. You're a woman – what do you see that I've missed? Perhaps there's something there that could lead me to her.'

'You really know nothing about her yet?'

'I know her name is Laure.' In the kitchen the pressure cooker began to hiss. 'I'll be back,' he said. The pot-au-feu was beginning to bubble. In a few minutes he would add the vegetables he had part-cooked the night before: carrots, potatoes, leeks, turnips, celery, and two marrow bones.

'It's signed!' cried Chloé.

Laurent smiled as he took the plate of vegetables out of the fridge. He had introduced his daughter to reading from a young age. They had progressed from Marcel Aymé's *Des Contes du Chat Perché* to Harry Potter, and from there to Edgar Allan Poe's short stories and then on to poetry – Baudelaire, Rimbaud, Prévert, Éluard – before returning to fiction and Proust, Stendhal,

Camus, Céline and others before finally tackling contemporary authors. If he had achieved one thing with Chloé's education, it was to instil in her a love of literature. Now Chloé made her own literary discoveries without his guidance. Recently she had been on a 'Mallarmé trip', declaring his epic poems 'better than Alain Baschung'.

He tasted the broth off the tip of the ladle, added a pinch of salt and then tipped in the vegetables. Twenty minutes on a low heat and they would be cooked to perfection. He opened a bottle of Fixin and poured himself a glass just as a text came through on his mobile. Dominique. She hadn't replied to his text of the evening before, nor the one two days earlier. 'See you this evening?' she had written. Laurent took a sip of wine. 'Having dinner with my daughter,' he texted back. There was no reply.

Chloé appeared in the doorway and leant against the door frame.

'Taste this,' he said, holding out his glass to her. 'Burgundy, Fixin, Reserve Monseigneur Alexandre 2009, a gift from a customer.'

She swirled the wine about and breathed in the aroma as he had taught her, then drank a mouthful, indicating her approval with a slight nod, just as her father did in restaurants.

'She must be in her forties,' began Chloé. 'Judging by her make-up, never mind her choice of chic designer bag. A thirty-year-old wouldn't choose that, and an old hag wouldn't even know about it.'

'Don't talk like that, Chloé. You're not at school any more. But go on,' said Laurent, taking another sip.

Chloé sighed, then continued, 'She's very attached to the past – the mirror is ancient, a family heirloom; perhaps it was her grandmother's. And she uses an unusual perfume – no one wears

Habanita any more – she writes weird things in her notebook, she has a book signed by an author you admire … ' Then she concluded with an ironic smile, 'She's the woman for you.'

'I expected more from you when I let you see the bag,' replied Laurent coldly.

'OK,' said Chloé, 'no need to get worked up. You're probably on the right track with the dry-cleaner's, but you can do much better than that.'

'I'm listening,' commented Laurent, attending to the cooker.

'You should go and see Modiano.'

When Laurent shrugged, she said, 'I'm serious, you have to ask him. He's the only one who's seen her, he must remember her.'

'I don't know Modiano, Chloé,' said Laurent, lowering the heat under the pressure cooker.

'But you know hundreds of writers. He lives here in Paris – surely you must have a way of reaching him?'

'I think he lives near the Luxembourg Gardens, but I don't have his address.'

'Ask his publisher.'

'Chloé, they would never give it to me.'

'You'll have to find a way, he's the key.' Chloé grabbed his wine glass from the table and took a sip.

'Are you in love?' she asked after a moment's silence.

'Who with?' replied Laurent, lifting the pressure-cooker lid.

'The woman with the red notebook.'

'Of course not. I'd just like to give her bag back. Bring the plates through.'

Chloé put the glass down and picked up the plates from the worktop. 'How's Dominique?' she asked quietly.

'She's not really speaking to me at the moment,' Laurent said gloomily.

'Did she see the handbag?' Chloé immediately asked.

'Why do you ask?'

'Because if she saw it she'll have freaked out.'

Laurent looked at her, ladle in the air.

'She might have been worried that you wanted to meet the woman,' amended Chloé, enunciating carefully.

Laurent served the pot-au-feu. 'Let's talk about something else.'

Two hours had passed. The pot-au-feu had been declared 'the best in the world' and the message to Dominique had remained unanswered. Chloé was now curled up on the sofa in socks and T-shirt. She was watching reality TV. Women city-dwellers had come to meet farmers with the rather dubious aim of seducing them and eventually settling down with them. Between the discovery of cows' udders and bucolic walks in the forest, the improbable couples revealed their feelings on camera, with no detail spared. How these men who lived in tiny remote villages, unable even to ride their mopeds in front of their neighbours' windows without being immediately identified, could expose their shameless, cringe-making pick-up attempts to millions of viewers was a mystery to Laurent.

'What I meant was ... I do really like you ...' were the timid words of one strapping lad with a crew cut.

'You do?' said the woman wonderingly. 'I'm very touched, Jean-Claude, but how can I put this ... Let's just be friends.' Then she added brightly, 'We could write to each other.'

The farmer had taken this hard. He'd stared out at the horizon of the Auvergne hills obviously not enthralled by the prospect of an epistolary relationship.

'Are you angry with me?' simpered the woman, with the same intonation as a mother refusing her offspring another biscuit.

'No, of course not,' muttered Jean-Claude.

'How long are you going to be watching that garbage?' asked Laurent.

'It's not garbage, I love it,' replied Chloé. Her mobile rang; her friend Charlène must be watching the same programme. 'You're right, totally, he looks like him, it is him,' cried Chloé before going off into hysterical laughter.

Laurent recalled his conversations with Pascal on their parents' phones when they had been at the lycée together. If there was one thing that defined adolescence it was hysterical laughter. You never laughed like that again. In adolescence the brutal realisation that the world and life were completely absurd made you laugh until you couldn't catch your breath, whereas in later life it would only result in a weary sigh.

From: Lecahierrouge@gmail.com
To: librairie_Pageapage@wanadoo.fr
Subject: Question
Good morning Jean,
Quick question – was it you who told me you often saw Modiano in the Luxembourg Gardens in the morning?
Laurent

From: librairie_Pageapage@wanadoo.fr
To: Lecahierrouge@gmail.com
Hi Laurent,
Yes, it was me. I saw him again last week. And your email is well timed. I see from Électre that you still have a copy of Paul Kavanski's *Éloge de la Beauté*. One of my regular customers is desperate for it today. Could you put it aside for me?

From: Lecahierrouge@gmail.com
To: librairie_Pageapage@wanadoo.fr
I've put the Kavanski behind the till for you. What time do you see Modiano and where exactly in the gardens?

From: librairie_Pageapage@wanadoo.fr

To:Lecahierrouge@gmail.com

I'll tell my customer to come and collect it; his name is Marc Desgrandschamps. Thank you! I usually see Modiano about 9 a.m. I often pass him in front of the Orangerie. Why do you ask?

'I'm not sure I can help you. I can't really remember ... Wait, yes ... I do remember something. Yes ... two weeks ago, perhaps a bit longer ... behind Odéon; it was raining; she stopped me in the street to ask me to ... sign her book. She took it out of her bag. She seemed a little shy, or ... ill at ease. No, that's not it either ... it was obvious she wasn't in the habit of doing that sort of thing; nor was I, for that matter. We were both of us a bit ... you know ... We weren't quite sure ... what to say to each other ... There was a rather wonderful yellow light, probably a storm coming ... She must have been about forty, she was wearing a sort of black raincoat, she had brown hair to her shoulders ... very light-coloured eyes, grey maybe ... and a pale complexion; she was very pretty. It was raining ... her face was wet ... she had a very beautiful smile, wasn't very tall, with a beauty spot to the right of her upper lip. She wore lipstick ... red, of course, but with a hint of coral and high-heeled shoes with straps. No tights ... at least ... that's what I remember.'

He paused. Laurent stared at him. Only Patrick Modiano could tell you he didn't remember the woman he had met in the street then immediately go on to give you a description that would have delighted any police force in the country. 'Thank you,' said Laurent in a low voice.

Modiano continued to look at him with that trademark

expression of concern. 'But now I wonder why you're asking ... and why you waited for me in the Luxembourg Gardens. Has something happened to her?'

Why indeed? Laurent preferred not to think about that too much. What's more he had had three espressos and a vin chaud at Le Rostand to give himself courage. It was the second day he had staked out the Luxembourg Gardens. He was like one of those passionate ornithologists who will watch a rare bird through their binoculars without even taking a photograph of it because the very sight of the creature is recompense enough for long days, or even long weeks of waiting. For Laurent, the rare bird was the winner of the 1978 Prix Goncourt. Yesterday, no Modiano had shown itself in the park and, on the stroke of nine-thirty, he had returned to his arrondissement. Today he had risen at dawn and had been hanging about the Orangerie since seven o'clock until the tall figure had appeared at the end of the path. Getting up from his bench, Laurent had experienced the racing heart of a true enthusiast finally setting eyes on the large-beaked warbler. Actually, it was even stronger than that: it was as if he had just spotted a specimen of the mythical dodo, unseen since the end of the eighteenth century.

The author of *Villa Triste* was ambling, hands in raincoat pockets, apparently looking towards some far-off point on the park horizon. A slight wind ruffled his now grey-white hair. Laurent, clutching a copy of *Accident Nocturne*, started to walk towards the author. He could not summon a suitable phrase with which to deflect Modiano from his onward path. He would have to start by catching the man's eye, he was thinking, when the writer's gaze met his own. Laurent smiled at him and was rewarded with a fleeting smile in return. Then the words seemed to speak themselves: 'Good morning, excuse me,' began Laurent as Modiano stepped imperceptibly aside like a startled pet preparing to flee when you move to stroke it. Laurent held out his copy of *Accident Nocturne* like an ID card, right in front of Modiano. 'Don't be alarmed,' he said, 'I just have a question to ask you. My name is Laurent Letellier; I'm a bookseller, but it's nothing to do with that. It's just that I'm trying to find someone.'

Patrick Modiano smoothed the collar of his raincoat and looked at Laurent in mild confusion. 'Oh? Yes, go on, I'm listening.'

Heart thumping, Laurent related the story of the bag he had found. 'Yes, I see ... a woman's handbag ... Abandoned ... just sitting there.' Anxiety started to show on Modiano's face, as if he were highly disturbed by the story of the bag and would not be able to sleep because of it. Laurent had just upset one of the greatest living writers because of his amateur investigation. He apologised several times and with each passing second became more and more aware of the absurdity of his inititiative, then just as he was wishing he could vanish into thin air, Modiano had responded, 'I'm not sure I can help you. I can't really remember ... Wait, yes ... I do remember something.'

Now they were walking side by side. 'Yes ... we must find her to give her back her bag ... that will complete the story,' Modiano mused. They exchanged some banalities about the weather and the upkeep of the gardens in winter.

'I haven't really been any help to you ...'

'Oh, you have, you've been a big help,' Laurent told him. 'And thank you, thank you for all your books.'

'Thank you,' Modiano murmured quietly, looking at him, then, 'Good luck with your search.'

They shook hands and Modiano added – purely out of politeness, Laurent felt sure – that he would perhaps drop into the bookshop one day if he were passing that way. Laurent watched him walk away. A breeze had sprung up again making the author's coat flap slightly. Then Modiano disappeared round the corner as though consumed by the railings.

He had done it. He had risen to his daughter's challenge. In the enthusiasm of the moment, Laurent decided to go on a tour of the nearby dry-cleaners'. It was Thursday; the strappy dress would be ready. When he got back to Le Cahier Rouge, he told Maryse and Damien that he would be gone a couple of hours. Having identified nine dry-cleaners' within a radius of roughly a kilometre, he printed out the Google map of the area, assiduously marked each dry-cleaner's with a little cross and set off on the trail. If he used the Métro as well as walking, he would get round them all by midday.

But at eleven o'clock precisely, ahead of schedule, he was walking along the street carefully carrying a hanger from which dangled a white dress in a transparent dry-cleaning bag marked *Aphrodite Dry-cleaner's: 'We care about caring for your clothes'*. He had visited six dry-cleaners'. The first four had told him the ticket was not one of theirs, the fifth had brought Laurent seven ironed Hermès ties. Although incontestably the crème de la crème of leather working, the famous design house produced, in Laurent's view, the most hideous ties in the world: motifs of foxes, snails, horses and little dogs on silk backgrounds of mustard and blue were spread out in front of him. His ticket's number, 0765, did indeed correspond to the ticket on the ties. But on learning that the ties were not what Laurent was after, the dry-cleaner quickly understood that the ticket was not in fact one of his. The woman in the sixth dry-cleaner's had taken the ticket, brought the dress without comment, and asked him for twelve euros. In reply to the question Laurent had been burning to ask, the answer had been as simple as it was disappointing: no, she had no recollection at all of the person who had dropped the dress off, sorry.

So now Laurent had a first name, and a description: shoulder-length brown hair, pale complexion, very light eyes, possibly grey, a beautiful smile, not very tall and with a beauty spot to the right of her upper lip. But nothing at all to indicate her surname. Although Laurent had been galvanised by his meeting with Modiano and was very proud of 'Operation Dry-cleaner', he was forced to admit that he had now played all his cards. Returning to his apartment, he hung the dress on the door of the bookcase, stepped back, then took the dress down and held it by his side. Judging Laure's approximate height, he held the dress well below the level of his shoulder. The glass door of the bookcase reflected back their image, like a daguerreotype of yesteryear in which the face and body of the woman had been effaced by time, leaving nothing but the image of the dress. The man had been preserved, a man and his phantom wife. Behind the glass you could see the spines of the novels Laurent collected, the old paperbacks, the first editions, the Pléiades classics, the books signed by authors who'd come to do events at Le Cahier Rouge. Although there were books elsewhere in the apartment, this was the bookcase where he displayed the books that meant the most to him. He even made sure not to shelve authors who did not get on next to each other. So he would never put Céline next to Sartre, or Houellebecq next to Robbe-Grillet. The image of him posing next to an empty dress could have been captioned *The Imaginary Girlfriend*, a title borrowed from John Irving.

(The book did not recount the tale of a bookseller who finds the bag of an unknown woman but was actually the memoirs of the student Irving, his first literature courses and his discovery of Greco-Roman wrestling.)

He hung the dress back on the bookcase and turned to the card table. Laid out were the little stones, the mirror, the make-up bag, the keys with their hieroglyphic fob attached, the *Pariscope*, the little notebook with her thoughts, the Modiano paperback, the Montblanc pen, the hair clip with the blue flower, the recipe for *ris de veau*, and the packet of liquorice sweets. He took one. He was not going to find her. The search was over. The thought of putting all those objects back in the bag and taking it to Rue des Morillons was as repellent as the idea of taking an animal to a rescue shelter on the pretext that you could no longer look after it. Laurent suddenly felt profoundly dejected. He seriously considered leaving Laure's possessions on the table for good. Like those knick-knacks that collect dust, family souvenirs brought back from holidays that end up being part of the decor. He switched off the light, and went back down to Le Cahier Rouge. In the gloom, the dress gave off an almost phosphorescent glow.

It was a terrible idea. An idea that only Dominique could have come up with. To meet up with other people rather than have dinner alone when they could have talked to each other, and he could have explained the story of the bag and the hairgrip and soothed her fears. She, however, wanted a neutral encounter in a neutral environment. In a new wine bar – Le Chantemuse – opened by a couple of graphic designers who had moved into bistronomy. There were to be seven guests: a couple of journalists – both remarried – who were celebrating their wood wedding anniversary (five years), an architect, a junior minister, a press officer and the two of them.

When he arrived, they were already seated at the back of the restaurant, each with a glass of green kir royale – which was apparently champagne with basil liqueur. Laurent kissed Dominique perfunctorily on the lips then greeted the other guests and sat down opposite her. Dominique seemed pleased to see him.

'We're waiting for Pierre, but I don't understand, he's not answering his mobile,' announced the junior minister with the annoyed air of one who juggles many case files and does not appreciate unforeseen problems.

Dominique suggested that since he was flying in from Madrid, maybe his flight had been cancelled; the female half of the anniversary couple hoped there had not been an accident; the press officer was more inclined to think that Pierre must have got the wrong date, then Laurent joined them all in toasting the wood anniversary of the couple he didn't know. The architect did not turn up and his chair remained empty all evening. Laurent imagined that Pierre had probably preferred to stay in Madrid and eat tapas with a flamenco dancer, but he decided not to share this opinion with his neighbours.

The conversation turned to the exhibitions that were currently on and to politics. From time to time he caught Dominique's eye. They held each other's gaze without saying anything, then turned away again. Their complicity during these fleeting exchanges seemed faked – it was a far cry from the look that had passed between them on the evening of the event at Le Cahier Rouge. That look in which they had promised each other, almost by telepathy, that nothing would stop them ending the night together. That had been a little over a year ago, which was a cotton anniversary, according to the wood anniversary couple. Would they celebrate the next anniversary together? As the dinner progressed, Laurent doubted it. Ephemeral relationships like that just happen, programmed from the outset to die after a brief period – but you only realise that as they are about to end.

After the starter of organic salmon with fair-trade red fruits, they moved on to steamed chicken fillets with vegetables (organic obviously) in a spicy sauce made from an ancestral Peruvian recipe brought back from a trip taken by one of the graphic designers-turned-restaurateurs. It was all very of the moment, very on trend, very *boho*. As Dominique talked about an article on the economic crisis she wanted to put together for *Le Monde*, Laurent fell to dreaming of those Relais et Châteaux hotels in the provinces where, in the dining rooms with crackling fires, they said 'Enjoy the rest of your meal' at every course.

'What's happened to your pretty handbag?' Dominique's question had involuntarily coincided with a lull in the conversation and Laurent was obliged to explain the saga of the handbag to the group.

'I would love it if a man searched for me like that,' declared the press officer, finishing off her third glass of wine. 'Perhaps it would end in a beautiful relationship. I'm so bored, stuck with Mark and the children.' Her remark struck a sour note. 'What?' she went on. 'It's the truth. After twenty-two years of marriage, you get tired of each other. I'm sorry but that's the way it is.'

Dominique asked her neighbour, the junior minister, if he would kindly refill her glass. Laurent reached for the bottle, but the other man beat him to it.

'Have you had a book signing with Jean Echenoz?' the wood anniversary wife asked, showing a sudden interest in his bookshop.

'Yes,' replied Laurent. 'For *Ravel*.'

'What was the name of his book that won the Goncourt?'

'*I'm Leaving*,' replied Laurent

'You also know Amélie Nothomb, Dominique tells me.'

'Yes, I know Amélie.'

The press officer asked him if the story she always told about eating rotten fruit was true. Laurent was at a loss. He had never discussed food with Amélie Nothomb. After that, everyone stopped asking him questions and the conversation took a different turn, ranging over relationships, family and children in no particular order. The voices round the table seemed to blend into one, dissolving into a gentle hubbub that Laurent was no longer listening to.

His gaze drifted to the architect's empty chair. He poured himself some more wine and smiled slightly, still looking at the chair. It seemed to him that by concentrating a little he could see a figure sketching itself in the air. Yes, as he emptied his glass, the figure became clearer. Purely by willpower he had conjured up a person sitting in that chair. He was the only one who could see her; she had shoulder-length brown hair, a pale complexion, very light eyes, a beauty spot to the right of her upper lip, lipstick, red of course but tending to the coral. She was as bored by this dinner as he was and now – there was no doubt about it – she was smiling at him. No one had noticed and their complicity was complete. If he were to concentrate even harder he would see her get up and come over to him. She would lean over and say into his ear, 'Come on, Laurent, let's go.'

'Are you coming with me?'

Laurent turned to look at Dominique.

'I'm going to smoke a cigarette – will you join me?'

Outside the cold took him by surprise as Dominique lit her cigarette, shielding herself from the wind. She took her first drag.

'I think we're drifting apart,' she said, after a silence.

'I agree,' replied Laurent quietly.

'I think you're seeing someone else.'

Laurent said nothing.

'You've been thinking about her all evening. It's obvious … I think this is the parting of the ways.'

Laurent thought, She should make a list of all her 'I thinks'.

Dominique moved towards him and ran her hand through his hair, with a disillusioned smile. 'Happy hunting, Laurent.' Then she added coldly, 'Don't ever call me again.' And she threw away her barely started cigarette and went back into the restaurant.

There, it was over. How was it so easy to disappear from someone else's life? Perhaps it was with the same ease that you enter it. A chance meeting, a few words exchanged, and a relationship begins. A chance falling out, a few words exchanged and that same relationship is over.

He had gone back in a few minutes later, but he longed to quietly pay his share and leave. How many things do we feel obliged to do for the sake of it, or for appearances, or because we are trained to do them, but which weigh us down and don't in fact achieve anything? Dominique wouldn't look at him any more. She was deep in conversation with the junior minister, who was smiling at her. Laurent wondered if he was looking at his replacement. He waited a good quarter of an hour without anyone talking to him, and it was certain now, the junior minister was making good progress, and, judging by her charming smiles, Dominique was responding to his advances. The title of Jean Echenoz's book was now an invitation he could no longer refuse.

Laurent rose and said, 'I'm leaving.'

As he walked away towards the till, he heard Dominique say, 'Ignore him. That would also make a good title for a book.'

On the stroke of seven Frédéric Pichier arrived at the bookshop where readers were already waiting. He took off his scarf and padded jacket, shook hands with each of the bookshop staff, said that he was 'really very touched' by Laurent's compliments on his book and let himself be led to the little table set up for him. He settled down behind the piles of *The Sky is our Frame* and some of his earlier books. Maryse brought him a glass of vin chaud and some savoury biscuits. There were at least forty people in the shop already and more were pushing through the door. Laurent sat down beside Pichier, smiled at the assembled customers, which immediately hushed the low murmuring amongst them and then raised his voice to thank both the author for kindly accepting the invitation from Le Cahier Rouge and the customers for coming out on this cold evening. He then introduced Frédéric Pichier, talking briefly about his work, his life and his latest book. The writer answered the questions about the book from his host, who had annotated the text with care. The session ended with applause from the audience and Laurent left the author to his signing. Damien served the customers with glasses of vin chaud and they obediently queued up in front of the author's table.

Laurent grabbed a glass of wine and went over to Maryse. 'It's good that so many people have turned up,' he murmured to her.

'And they're still coming,' she replied, looking over at the door. 'Isn't your friend Dominique joining us?'

'Dominique won't be coming any more, Maryse,' replied Laurent, staring at the cinnamon stick floating in his wine.

'I'm sorry, Laurent. I shouldn't have said anything.'

'No, it doesn't matter, really it doesn't,' he told her, taking her hand. 'I've met someone else,' he added, wondering in the next instant what had come over him.

Pichier was listening with a smile to the compliments of one of the customers, Françoise, and replying to the usual questions: 'How did you get the idea?' 'How long did it take you to write?' 'You must have had to do a huge amount of research.' Then, as he was finishing off his dedication, 'For Françoise, my loyal reader ...' she reluctantly asked him the ritual question, 'Are you working on a new novel?' 'Yes, yes, I'm working on something ...' replied Pichier laconically.

The truth was that for the last two and a half months he had been adrift in a plot he himself described as crap to his friends and family, and which he had avoided relaying to his editor. It was the story of a young maid in the 1900s set against a wide backdrop that ranged from rural French society to the upper classes in Paris. And it depicted the purest souls as well as the slightly depraved elite of the Belle Époque. He was stuck on page 40. Marie, the young serving girl, was having an affair with a brutish but romantic butcher's boy, while the son of the family, a timid aesthete who collected beetles, was secretly fantasising about her. Sometimes in his giddier moments, Pichier told himself he was going to give birth to a monster, that he would be the first to produce a novel that was part J.-K. Huysmans and part Marc Levy. Some afternoons, he wished that his heroine would end up at the hands of the knackers of Les Halles. As for the well-born young virgin, many a time had he itched to send him off to the Trappist monks. Sometimes, when he was in real trouble, he wrote barely three sentences before spending the rest of the day in front of his screen, surfing the web, especially eBay, looking for objects that, of course, could not be found. He also spent time, like all his fellow writers, typing his name and the title of his books into search engines, looking for reviews on blogs and literary sites, smiling when he came across a good review and cursing when he came across a mixed one that ended with the insulting phrase, 'This book did not make much of an impression on me.' Sometimes, using a pseudonym, he would write a review himself on Fnac.com or Amazon.com, praising himself and hailing the great talent of Frédéric Pichier. Recently he had even gone as far as to write, under the identity 'Mitsi', on Babelio.com, 'Pichier, a future Goncourt winner?'

Like many writers, Pichier had another job. He was a year eleven and twelve French teacher. At the Lycée Pablo-Neruda in the outer suburbs, which was next door to the Robespierre nursery school. After twenty-one years' teaching, he had felt a sense of exhaustion creeping in. Nervous exhaustion. Encouraged by his nearest and dearest and by his editor, he had taken a year's 'sabbatical', so that he could devote himself exclusively to his writing. Now, suffering from writer's block, alone every day at home, he regretted the decision that had deprived him of his pupils. They might have been rowdy, sly, complicated, and lacking in culture, sometimes appallingly so, but he had to admit that his days with them had been vastly more entertaining than those he now spent in front of his screen. Their concept of literature was frequently disconcerting. To them the Marquise de Merteuil was a sort of 'cougar' and Valmont 'too sick'. They had spent a month going through the text as if it were a TV series. He had chopped it into extracts: season one, season two ... of *Les Liaisons Dangereuses*. They had really liked the title; they thought it sounded sexy and subversive, both attributes that aroused their curiosity. In their own fashion, they had actually followed the thoughts of the eighteenth-century author. *Madame Bovary* had just been, for most of the boys, 'lame' with a totally desperate heroine. The girls, however, seemed to understand the woes of Emma a bit better. As for the mining community in *Germinal*, the entire class might as well have been reading science fiction. *Un Amour de Swann* with its ending, 'To think that I've wasted years of my life, that I've longed to die, that I've experienced my greatest love, for a woman who didn't appeal to me, who wasn't even my type!' awakened more interest. Some of the boys seemed to find a connection between Proust's thoughts and their personal experience of disappointment in love. 'The hero was really into a top bird who just wasn't right for him. He finally realised it and that made him think a lot about himself and his life' was Hugo's brilliant summing up – fourteen out of twenty – 'Good comprehension of the text, but your analysis is underdeveloped and watch your spelling, Hugo.' Some pupils, mainly girls, had read *The Sky is our Frame*. Djamila had even asked him to sign her copy and asked him lots of pertinent questions about the structure of the book, which had both touched him and made him feel optimistic.

The author signed and smiled politely at his readers, drinking down several vins chauds. Laurent went over to ask if everything was all right.

'Yes, excellent,' replied Pichier.

'We've sold thirty copies,' Laurent murmured to him.

Pichier nodded.

'Hello,' he said to a new customer as she approached. 'Hello ... Nathalie,' he added with a friendly smile, looking at her neckline.

'How do you know my name?' exclaimed the customer.

Pichier smiled, pleased with the effect he had produced.

'You're wearing it round your neck,' he said, narrowing his eyes.

She put her hand up to a gold pendant. 'You read hieroglyphics?' she said admiringly.

'I wrote *Tears of Sand*,' responded Pichier, laying his hand on a copy. 'There's a lot about Egypt in it. I learnt as I was doing research for the book.'

'I'll be right back,' said Laurent quickly and he made his way through the customers to the internal door of the bookshop that led to the lobby of the apartment building. He took the stairs four at a time up to his flat, opened the door, turned the light on, quickly grabbed the keys from the card table, and looked breathlessly at the fob with the hieroglyphics. Now he understood: it had never been meant for keys, it was a pendant just like the customer's; it was simply that she had attached it to her key ring. He left the apartment, slamming the door behind him and rushed back down the stairs.

The customer was having two books signed: *Tears of Sand* for her husband and the latest novel for herself. Pichier was polishing off the dedication as Laurent approached. He had to wait while the customer related a colourful family anecdote, something that had happened to her great-grandmother during the Great War which was very like an episode in the novel. At last she said goodbye to the author and Laurent slipped in front of the next customer.

'Can I just interrupt a moment,' he said to Pichier. 'Do you know what this says?' And he laid the bunch of keys on the cover of one of the books.

Pichier picked it up, adjusted his glasses and looked closely at the Egyptian characters. 'Yes ...' he murmured. 'It says Laure ...' Then he turned the little rectangle over. '...Va ... Vala ... Valadier.'

Laure Valadier.

Silence is golden. The phrase inscribed above the entrance of the ateliers and gold-plated by Alfred Gardhier (1878–1949) himself had taken on a new significance for William. It had been four days now, and Laure had still not woken up. No matter what Professor Baulieu said to reassure him – the brain scan had not shown any damage – the fact that she was still in a coma surely did not bode well. He picked up the leaf with the flat of his knife, placed it on the calfskin cushion and blew very gently; it unfurled into a perfect rectangle. With the sharp edge of the knife, he divided it in two, rubbed the sable brush against his cheek and picked up the first half in one smooth movement. The static electricity lifted the leaf above the layer of wetted Armenian bole covering the woodwork. With a flick of the wrist he dropped it into place. In a fraction of a second, the gold leaf moulded perfectly to the contours of the wood, blending in with the seventy-five others he had already positioned that day. Two more and the restoration of the pier glass bearing the coat of arms of the Counts of Rivaille would be all but complete. The only thing left was to burnish the surface with an agate stone until the gold shone as it had in its glory days.

For the last four days Laure's seat in the workshop had been vacant. When she had not arrived on Thursday morning, he had known something was wrong. At eleven o'clock he left her a message. At midday he left another. At one o'clock he rang her landline. After lunch, during which Laure's absence was the main subject of conversation with Agathe, Pierre, François, Jeanne and Amandine – the other gilders who had completed their apprenticeships – he agreed with Sébastien Gardhier (the fourth generation to run the family business) that it would be sensible if he went round to see her.

'It's William again. I've left work. I'll just go home and pick up Belphégor's keys and then I'm coming round' was the last message he had left on Laure's mobile. This was how they referred to the spare set of keys to her apartment; William only used them to go in and feed the cat when she was away.

When he had rung the bell twice and no one had come to the door, he made up his mind to let himself in. As soon as the door opened, the cat slipped out onto the landing, as he had a habit of doing. He looked at William, arched his back and started moving crabwise, his ears pointing backwards. 'He does that when he's scared – it's an attacking position.' Laure's words came into his head, and if the cat was scared it must mean something had happened.

'Laure?' he called out. 'Are you home?'

As soon as he stepped inside, he had a strong sense of déjà vu. The scene in front of him was merging with one he had seen before, as he suddenly remembered the afternoon he had let himself into his grandmother's house when she had not come to the door. That afternoon, ten years ago, when she had not responded to him asking if she was there, as he was doing now. He had gone round opening doors and found every room empty until he reached the kitchen. She was lying on the tiled floor. Lifeless.

'Laure?' he shouted, opening the door to her bedroom and

then the study, the bathroom, the toilet and finally, at the end of the corridor, the kitchen. This time the apartment really was empty, and William sat himself down on the sofa in the sitting room. He concentrated on his breathing; his chest felt tight and wheezy and the telltale itch was creeping up his back. He took out his inhaler, held it to his mouth and pressed twice. Belphégor slid between William's legs, brushing him with his tail.

'Where is Laure? Do you know?' asked William. But the animal remained silent.

Having stroked the cat and established that nothing in the flat appeared untoward, William made one last call to Laure's mobile and got her voicemail again. He left a brief message before closing the door behind him and heading back downstairs. On the face of it, no, nothing untoward, but something must have happened, something big, for her to have failed to turn up for work and not be answering her phone. If he hadn't heard from her by the end of the day, he would call the police. When he reached the lobby, he saw that a white envelope had been pushed under the main door. He was sure it had not been there when he arrived. He leant down and read the delicate handwriting: Mademoiselle Laure Valadier and family.

Hotel Paris Bellevue ***

Madame, Monsieur,

Should you require any information about Laure Valadier, who stayed with us on the night of 15 January and was taken ill, please contact reception.

Kind regards,

The management

That evening, they had let him see her through a window. She was lying in a room shared with several others. The patient next to her was hooked up to a ventilator. Laure seemed just to be asleep with a drip in her arm. When he returned the next day he was allowed to sit at her bedside. Her face was relaxed, her eyelids closed. Her breathing was barely perceptible, in and out at regular intervals. The hushed room was bathed in weak artificial light. There were six beds he now counted, and the men and women lying in them were all deep in the kind of sleep that goes on for days, weeks, years, or even until the end of their lives, leaving loved ones to wonder: was he aware he was dying, or was he already long gone? The only sound was the quiet pumping of the ventilator by the neighbouring bed, which went on continuously as if it had a life of its own which would never end. The human race could die out, mortal bodies turn to dust, and this pump would go on gently rising and falling until the end of time.

'It's William,' he finally murmured. 'I'm here. Apparently people in comas can still hear. I don't know if that's true. Don't worry, I'm looking after Belphégor. He's eating his Virbac biscuits, the duck ones. Amandine and Pierre took over your work today; they'll finish restoring the Virgin Mary for you.'

He placed his hand over hers. It didn't move.

'I have to go to Berlin soon to do the ceiling for the German guy – Schmidt or Schmirt, is it? – you know, the gold mouldings.'

I'm scared of storms.

'I'll think of a plan for the cat. I'll think of something, don't worry.'

I'm scared of zoos. I'm scared because the animals are in cages.

'You have to wake up. You have to come back, Laure.'

I'm scared of boats.

'All this for a bag. I told you not to buy it, it was too nice.'

I'm scared when I don't understand. I don't understand why I'm here.

I'm scared when I don't know where I am, and I don't know where I am. I don't know 'when' I am.

I'm scared when William talks to me and I can't say anything back.

The days had passed between visits to Laure in the morning and Belphégor at night. Professor Baulieu had taken him into his office.

'Your sister ... She is your sister, isn't she?'

The doctor had a sweep of white hair, a rather round face and kind, laughing eyes. The ability to keep a degree of detachment and a sense of humour must be essential in this job, William thought to himself.

'What do you think?' he replied, smiling ruefully.

'I think ... you're not her brother,' the doctor said with a knowing smile. 'But that's really neither here nor there. What matters is that you're here, which is great, and you're the only one able to speak for her.'

William replied as best he could to the doctor's questions. Yes, he was effectively Laure's next of kin; she had lost her husband and parents and had no children – only a sister who lived a long way away, in Moscow, from whom she heard only once or twice a year.

'She has a lot of friends, though,' William began explaining.

'Including you,' the doctor cut in, 'the best of them, the only one who's here. You must talk to her when you come. That's very important. She can hear you.'

'I do talk to her.'

'That's good,' the doctor said, nodding approvingly. 'Right, let me tell you where we are. Laure is in a mild form of coma caused by the head injury and the subdural haematoma that developed during the night. This sometimes happens to people involved in car crashes – they go home feeling a bit dazed and collapse an hour later. The signs are encouraging. I see no cause for concern – she should wake up within days. It seems she was mugged,' he said, consulting the notes on his desk.

'She had her bag stolen. I guess she must have tried to fight back,' replied William.

The doctor shook his head with a sigh. 'All for a handful of euros, and I've seen far worse,' he muttered.

William went on to answer a series of questions about Laure: Was he aware of any previous operations? Was she on any medication? Had she ever been involved in an accident? Any drug or alcohol addictions? If at all possible, he should also get hold of her social security number and a few other bits of paperwork. William said yes, he could supply that information – the ateliers would provide the necessary documents.

'Profession?' asked the doctor.

'Gilder,' replied William.

Baulieu looked up.

'Applying gold leaf to wood, metal or plaster,' William elaborated. 'Anything from an old picture frame to the dome of Les Invalides.'

'I take it you work together?'

'Correct,' mumbled William.

'That's interesting work. How many gold leaves does it take to do the dome of Les Invalides?' asked the doctor without looking up from his notes.

'Five hundred and fifty-five thousand.'

William let his gaze wander about the room. As in all surgeries, there were a handful of perplexing 'personal touches' that made you wonder why the doctor had chosen them as a back-drop to his consultations. They were usually blandly inoffensive, with vaguely artistic connotations: paperweights, statuettes, antique inkwells, mortars … William's eye was drawn to a white marble head mounted on a plinth on the doctor's desk.

'That's a Cycladic head on your desk.'

'Yes,' Baulieu replied, keeping his head down.

'Is it linked to your work?'

'Follow that thought,' the doctor said softly.

'It has no eyes, because your patients can't see. No mouth, because they can't talk. Just the nose to breathe through.'

The doctor looked up at William and ran his hand over the marble.

'Four thousand years of silence,' he murmured. 'You'll get your friend back, try not to worry.

'And get some rest – you look done in,' Baulieu said, before seeing him out.

Biscuits for Belphégor and a Martini Rosso for him. William stood in the kitchen in silence. He was leaving for Berlin the next morning and still had not managed to find anyone to feed the cat. There was no one he could really trust to take care of the keys and, more importantly, the pet. None of his friends would bother trekking across Paris to feed a cat. He would just have to leave bowls of food scattered about the flat and let Belphégor feed himself while he was gone. He knew Laure considered this something to be avoided at all costs because the cat was liable to eat everything in one go and then sick it all up. But he could see no other option. After draining another glass of Martini, he lined up the bowls on the worktop and was preparing to fill them under Belphégor's watchful gaze, when the doorbell rang.

Brown hair. Jeans and black loafers. White shirt. The man in the dark coat and blue scarf looked very surprised to find him there.

'Hello ...' said William.

'Hello ...' replied Laurent. There was a pause and then he cautiously continued. 'I've come to see Laure ... Laure Valadier.'

The cat came out onto the landing to greet him. Laurent knelt down. 'Hello, Belphégor,' he said, smiling and stroking the cat. The animal turned gracefully to wrap his tail around Laurent's hand.

'Are you a friend of Laure's?'

Laurent looked up at William. 'Not a friend exactly. I'm not sure how to put it ...' he said, looking embarrassed.

He was about to launch into a lengthy explanation but William stopped him.

'It's OK, I won't ask. I think I know who you are. She mentioned she'd met someone ... Come in. You've met the cat, so you must know your way around. I'm William, a friend of Laure's – we work together.'

'Laurent.'

The two men shook hands and the door closed behind them.

He had planned for everything, except this. A man with cropped bleached hair and a mildly eccentric dress sense opening the door and inviting him in. Since he had learnt her name, Laurent had called Laure's home number several times. She was in the phone book and he had located the only Laure Valadier in town with a few clicks online. As he suspected, she lived only a few streets away from where he had found the bag. The first time he dialled the number he anticipated various potential outcomes: that she would pick up, that a man would pick up – her husband, perhaps – that it would be engaged, that a child would pick up, that it would go through to her voice on an answer phone, that it would go through to a pre-recorded computer voice on an answer phone. Which is what happened. Laurent left no message. He repeated the process several days in a row. With false jollity, the computer voice told him over and over he could leave his message after the tone and save it with the hash key. No one ever picked up. So he composed a carefully worded letter instead. He settled down to write it after shutting the bookshop, and as he did so it struck him it had been a very long time since he last wrote a letter. After three pages of description detailing how he had found the bag, including apologies for looking inside it, explanations of the many paths his search had led him down, and ending on the story of how the mystery of the key ring had been solved by a French author doing a signing at his bookshop, Laurent felt totally spent. The work that had gone into producing three pages he was satisfied with – writing, rereading, revising, choosing every word and turn of phrase, crossing sections out, going back to change a verb and then an adjective further on – only increased his respect for writers.

It was a Haussmann-era six-storey building with the traditional golden stone façade and zinc roof. Laurent had come armed with Laure's keys to get through the heavy glass and black-iron door. So he would use the security fob and leave his envelope in the letter box marked Laure Valadier, which he knew he would find somewhere near the entrance. He looked for it among the wall of brushed-steel boxes, probably dating from the 1970s, on which the names of all the building's occupants were displayed. Larnier, Jean-Pierre – ground floor, right. Françon, Marc and Eugénie – 2nd floor, left (no junk mail please). C. Bonniot – 3rd floor, right. Dirkina Communications – 2nd floor, right. Dental surgery – 1st floor, left. Lecharnier-Kaplan – 4th floor, right. Laure Valadier – 5th floor, left.

As he went to slide the envelope through the opening, he hesitated. Had he come all this way, and gone to quite a lot of trouble, just to put a letter in a slot? There was an aroma of pot-au-feu floating in the air. By this time of the evening just about everyone was home from work. Through the door of the ground-floor flat he could hear a television tuned to a 24-hour news station. He heard laughter coming through the wall upstairs. This was ridiculous. Was he really going to head back out into the dark on his own and wait around for the phone to ring? Five floors up, Laure might be at home tonight. With shoulder-length brown hair, fair skin, light-coloured eyes – grey, perhaps – and a beauty spot to the right of her upper lip. Laurent was too close to stop now. He put the envelope back in his coat pocket and called the lift. The kind of museum piece found only in old Parisian apartment blocks rattled down. It had little wooden swing doors and the panel recording the floors dating from the 1930s. He pressed the black Bakelite button marked '5'. The cabin clattered shut and carried Laurent upwards to the sound of screeching pulleys. The entrance to the fifth-floor, left-hand apartment was dimly lit by a tulip-shaped lamp on the landing. There was no name on the door, just a little braided silver doorbell. So here he was. He would ring the bell and she would come to the door. Laurent ran his hand through his hair, cleared his throat and rang the bell.

William answered.

'I rang several times but no one picked up so I came round to leave a note,' said Laurent, taking the envelope out of his coat pocket.

William looked at him.

'So you don't know ... No, of course, you couldn't have known,' he said, flustered.

'Is there something I should know?' Laurent murmured.

'Take off your coat and sit down. Will you have a drink of something – whisky, vodka, orange juice, Martini Rosso? I'm on Martini.'

'Martini then,' said Laurent.

'Perfect, I'll be right back.'

William disappeared off down the corridor. Laurent hung his coat on the hook in the entrance hall.

The hall was dimly lit and on one of the walls he noticed a series of landscape oil paintings. These small pictures, dating from the nineteenth century, had been hung above a pedestal table. Bucolic lake or forest scenes with one thing in common: the absence of people. Just the natural setting and an impression of silence. Above the paintings, there was a box frame containing one of those metallic-blue butterflies whose name was on the tip of his tongue. On the table, a dish held a dozen golden antique keys. He picked one up. It was just like any other key that might have opened doors in days gone by, only it had been gold-plated, as had all the others in the bowl. Laurent thought of Bluebeard and the golden key that opened the door to the room of dead wives. Hearing William's footsteps coming back down the corridor, he put it back.

'There you go. I filled it halfway and put two ice cubes in – I hope that's how you take it.'

Both men sat in the sitting room, Laurent on the sofa and William facing him on a chair.

'Laure's fine,' he began, before immediately back-pedalling. 'Well, what I mean is … it could have been a lot worse. When did you last see her?'

Laurent pretended to think about it.

'Don't worry, it's not important,' cut in William. 'Something happened on the night of the 15th. Sorry, I'm not being very clear, but what I can tell you is that Laure was mugged. She had her bag stolen, she hurt her head, she's in a coma at the moment, but they think she'll wake up.'

'She's in a coma?' Laurent echoed.

'Yes, and she's taking her time waking up, but it should only be a matter of days now. I saw the doctor again yesterday and he's confident.'

'So that's why no one answered the phone …'

'Yes, and her mobile's missing, of course, along with her wallet and her bank card. They've taken two thousand euros out of her account; I found out when I rang the bank, but it should be covered by her insurance, and anyway that's not what matters.'

'No, it's not what matters,' mumbled Laurent.

'The important thing is that she wakes up,' William went on. 'I'll give you the details of the hospital and the ward she's on.'

'I don't know if I'll be allowed to visit, I'm not really family,' Laurent said awkwardly.

'Neither am I.' William shrugged. 'Anyway, now that she doesn't have her parents or husband any more, she doesn't have any family as far as I can tell, apart from her sister who lives in Moscow, and her friends.'

'You're right,' said Laurent. 'No husband any more,' he repeated.

'She told you about it?'

Laurent took a chance. 'Yes.'

William shook his head and took a gulp of Martini.

'It took her a long time to get over it.'

Laurent said nothing.

'You met her quite recently?' William went on.

'Yes, not long ago ...'

Laurent let his gaze wander around the living room, taking in the frames and books, a fireplace filled with logs waiting to be lit, a Venetian glass ceiling light, a modern lamp, a large mirror with a very elaborate gold frame.

'Where? If you don't mind me asking ...'

'In my bookshop. I'm a bookseller.'

'That makes sense,' William smiled. 'A few weeks ago, she bumped into a well-known author. She happened to have one of his books in her bag and asked him to sign it for her – she must have told you about that.'

'Yes, it was Modiano, near Odéon; it was raining.'

'Exactly. We were finishing off a project at the Senate. You seem like a nice person – I'm glad,' William added after a pause.

Laurent got up.

'Sorry, I just need to stretch my legs.'

'Yes, of course,' murmured William.

Laurent went over to look at a large framed photo. William and Laure were standing at the highest point of the roof of the

94

Opéra Garnier. Dressed in overalls, they were perched either side of the statue of Apollo holding up his golden lyre to the avenue below. They were both pointing at the lyre as they smiled at the camera.

At last, Laurent could see her face. Laure's hair was swept back by the wind, and it was possible to tell that her eyes were a light colour. There was the beauty spot to the right of her upper lip, and a chain around her neck with the hieroglyphic pendant hanging from it. She had delicate hands and wore a blue bracelet around her wrist. Now the mist had lifted and her features were in sharp focus. Her face was both different and very similar to the one he had imagined.

'I've got a copy of the same picture at my place,' said William. 'It was taken a few years ago. We did half of Apollo's lyre each.'

Next to the photo was another, smaller one of Laure, this time surrounded by five colleagues. They were all standing on the roof at Versailles, holding up their tools. She was wearing black sunglasses. Here again, there was gilding all around. It was beginning to make sense to Laurent: the keys in the entrance hall, the monuments, the job at the Senate William had mentioned. What they all had in common was gold.

'She doesn't wear the pendant with the hieroglyphics any more,' remarked Laurent.

'She attached it to her keys instead,' said William, swallowing another mouthful of Martini. 'It was a gift from a client in Egypt eight or ten years ago. Everyone who worked on the job got their full name spelt out in hieroglyphics. I lost mine. We've been all over the place together; she taught me everything I know. Laure's the best gilder out there.'

'Laure,' whispered Laurent, but whether he meant to say her name or that of the metal, *l'or*, he wasn't quite sure.

'Listen, I'm really sorry to ask,' William went on, 'but I have to go to Berlin for a couple of days, for work. Is there any chance you could look after Belphégor?'

Looking for a woman to return a handbag was one thing, settling down in her flat when she wasn't there, with her cat on his lap was another. The evening after William had asked him, he had opened the apartment door with the spare key William had given him – unnecessary since he already had the original. After giving the cat his food in the kitchen, Laurent poured himself a Jack Daniel's. He swallowed a mouthful of the smoky-tasting liquid. The bourbon warmed him up, filtering through his veins and relaxing his muscles. He went through to the sitting room and looked around, feeling as if he were there clandestinely or rather as if he were not really there at all. There are places where it is so peculiar to find yourself that you can't help thinking that your mind is playing tricks on you – that you are daydreaming and will soon wake up. What if there were another Laurent? A Laurent who was at home right now, in the apartment above the bookshop attending to his daily chores: replying to emails, preparing dinner, reading a new book.

Laure's apartment, with its sitting room and its deep sofa, its parquet floor covered with rugs and its carefully positioned lighting, was a delicious cocoon. In front of one of the windows there was a weeping fig whose branches stretched to the fireplace. Belphégor had happily adopted his evening visitor. He ate up his duck-flavoured cat food, then settled unhesitatingly on Laurent's lap, immobilising him on the sofa. It's an honour that cats bestow on you, as he was all too aware, his daughter's cat Putin never having deigned to sit on anyone – the most you could hope for was an intense stare that was vaguely reminiscent of his namesake in the Kremlin.

Before the cat had bestowed this honour, Laurent had wandered about the sitting room. The impression of 'reading a letter that's not addressed to you', as Guitry put it, was even stronger than when he had opened the bag. The apartment was itself like a sort of giant bag with thousands of nooks and crannies, each one containing a tiny portion of its occupant's life. Carrying his glass of bourbon, Laurent had gone from one object to another and from the table to the photograph. One section of wall was entirely taken up with a large bookcase with several shelves which held nothing but art books – some of them recent, others very old ones that she must have collected over the years. Architecture, painting – gilding of course – but also sale-room catalogues. At the end of one shelf there were several books by Sophie Calle, including one of her poetic masterpieces, *Suite Vénitienne*.

In 1980, for purely artistic reasons, Sophie had decided to follow men in the street randomly and without their knowledge. On these long perambulations, like a private detective, she took black-and-white pictures of the men from the back in various locations. Strangers that she followed for entire afternoons. One day she had spotted a new prey, but he escaped her and disappeared into the crowd. That evening by chance the man was introduced to her at a dinner. He told her that he would soon be going to Venice. Secretly Sophie Calle decided to resume her tailing of him – to follow him incognito even down the little alleyways and *rii* of Venice. From that escapade Sophie had created a logbook of 79 pages and 105 black-and-white pictures, with an afterword by Jean Baudrillard. Sophie's shadowing had come to an end when the man had turned round, recognised her and spoken to her. Although it didn't quite end there, because Sophie arranged to get to the station in Paris a few minutes before him to take a last picture. But all the tension and magic of the quest had vanished the moment they had spoken. The return to reality had signalled the end of the affair.

Laure owned a first edition – very difficult to find and also very expensive. Novels occupied another shelf. Laurent noticed several Modianos, some of them small paperbacks, some of them large format. Just to make sure, he pulled some of them out to check whether any of them were signed. There were also thrillers – English, Swedish, Icelandic – and Amélie Nothomb's books, several Stendhals, two Houellebecqs, three Echenozes, two Chardonnes, four Stefan Zweigs, five Marcel Aymés, everything by Apollinaire, an old hardback of *Nadja* by Breton, a paperback of Machiavelli's *The Prince*, then some Le Clézio, a dozen Simenons, three Murakamis, and a few of Jirô Taniguchi's graphic novels. The books were in no particular order, Jean Cocteau's *Poésies* sat next to Tonino Benacquista's *Saga*, which in turn was beside Jean-Philippe Toussaint's *La Salle de Bain*, then there was a very thick leather-bound book with gold lettering on the spine. Laurent took it down from the shelf.

It was a photo album, probably at least a hundred years old, with thick, gold-edged pages. The first photographs were from the 1920s, showing men with pencil moustaches and women in the outfits and hairstyles of the era. *Uncle Edward, Aunt Florence, family reunion – Christmas 1937* had been written in pencil under the pictures. The twentieth century advanced with the pages. In one photo from the 1970s a little girl with light-coloured eyes stared into the camera. She was holding a soft toy, a fox, and a Siamese cat was watching her. The little girl had a beauty spot above her upper lip. *Laure with young Sarbacane and Foxy.* Laure with her parents, Laure as a young girl, Laure on holiday with her sister Bénédicte. Laurent felt he had no right to be turning these pages, yet the desire to see the now familiar face in each of the photos was too strong for him. He was about to close the album, when he came to the last page. After that there was nothing; everything ended in 2007 with an article clipped from a newspaper. The article showed a picture of a man with short hair smiling as he posed beside the Afghan leader Ahmad Shah Massoud. 'Xavier Valadier (1962–2007), our colleague and friend, was killed in Iraq on 7 December. Xavier Valadier's photographs were viewed the world over …' The text ended with 'We will never forget you, Xavier, and our thoughts are with your family.' This was the man that William had referred to, and who was in one of the photographs in the envelope he'd found in the bag. Laurent put the album back in its place and went into the adjoining room.

The study was in darkness and he felt for the light switch. Fluorescent lighting flickered above a shelf high on the wall then stabilised. He saw other shelves with many DVDs and even some old videos, a large flat screen sitting on the floor and on the mantelpiece a CD player and a turntable. Thirty-three-inch records and CDs were piled up on the parquet. There was a mixture of classical music, rock and pop. No separation of genres here either; David Bowie was with Rubinstein, Radiohead and Devendra Banhart with Glenn Gould and Perlman. In the large mirror over the mantelpiece, postcards from all over the world were stuck between the gilt frame and the glass. Laurent did not touch any of them. On the desk, a computer and its keyboard, a jumble of pens and a notepad. A collection of twenty dice, all showing six. A roll of the dice will never eliminate chance, murmured Laurent just as a soft shadow passed between his legs. The cat. Who immediately jumped onto the black leather desk chair, then onto the table, nudged Laurent's face with his nose, then looked down at the lined-up dice. With the tip of his paw, he pushed two of them onto the floor, then looked at Laurent and immediately did the same with the next two dice.

'Don't do that, stop now,' Laurent told him, kneeling down to pick up the dice. The cat continued to push them with the end of his paw as soon as Laurent retrieved them. 'No, no, we're not going to play that game,' chided Laurent. He took the cat in his arms, closed the study door and then put him down again. The cat invited him to follow him to his mistress's bedroom. The room was all white, in contrast to the rest of the apartment, and its diffuse feeble light gave it the look of an igloo. An old wardrobe, a framed photograph of a red sky. On the radiator there was a toy fox, a little shabby, obviously the 'Foxy' of the photograph. The cat jumped up on the bedspread to show that it was also his bed and that he had the right to curl up on it whenever he wanted, which he proceeded to demonstrate. Together they visited the bathroom, with its black and gold enamel tiles. And on the shelves dozens of bottles, beauty products, creams and shampoos. Laurent picked up Pschitt Magique: 'New-generation micro peeling with biological action and no abrasive particles – transform your skin texture in exactly twenty seconds'. He put it down to breathe in the scent of a black bottle of Habanita. His eyes were wandering over this private intimate universe when his mobile rang, causing the cat to streak off towards the sitting room.

'Your daughter is telling me you put five cloves in the onion when you make pot-au-feu. I say you only need three and Bertrand agrees with me. So,' Clare added, sounding exasperated, 'as this seems to be extremely important right now, please can you confirm how many cloves you use?'

'Put her on,' replied Laurent calmly. 'Chloé? ... You need four cloves.'

'You need five, I was right!' shrieked Chloé.

'Chloé, I said four,' corrected Laurent.

'But I always have to be right,' she murmured.

Laurent closed his eyes and sighed. 'Chloé ... I'm at Laure's.'

'Wait, I'm walking away, they're arguing. Are you with her?'

'No, I'll explain – I'm feeding her cat.'

'So you found her?'

'Not exactly.'

'What's her name?'

'Valadier, Laure Valadier.'

'Is she pretty?'

'I've only seen her in photos. She's a gilder.'

'What is that, a gilder?'

'She adds gold decoration to things, gold leaf on frames, and monuments.'

'Too cool!' Chloé said enthusiastically. 'Wait, they're calling me. I'll have to go. Tell me all about it over dinner on Thursday,' and she promptly hung up.

When Laurent went home his apartment struck him as empty and silent in a way he had never felt before.

The second evening he again poured himself a Jack Daniel's and lit the fire. William rang, as they had agreed, on Laure's landline 'at cat time'. When he asked if Laurent had been to see her, Laurent had replied: 'Yes'. This time the question had obliged him to move to the next level, that of the outright lie. Then Laurent had settled down on the sofa and the cat had installed itself on his lap and started to purr as he stroked it gently. He told himself that this could not go on, that he had crossed the line some time ago. From having performed a fine act of citizenship (as the police put it), he was now sitting by Laure's open fire, which effectively made him guilty of breaking and entering. His amateur investigation had worked like a dream and when it came to an end – which it inevitably would – he would wonder whether these past few days had actually happened. For now, he felt reassured by the unfamiliar decor with its soft lighting and had no desire to return home. He had not experienced such a sense of peace for many years; time seemed to have been reduced to the rhythm of the crackling fire. Just as he was falling asleep he persuaded himself that he could spend the rest of his days here on this sofa, a black cat asleep on his lap, waiting for an unknown woman to wake up and return.

He found himself on the terrace of the tower at La Défense. It was a bad dream that recurred every two or three years. A dream that wasn't exactly a dream. The terrace must still exist. It was from another life. A life in which he was Laurent Letellier – wealth adviser – private banking. A life which had ended on the thirty-fourth floor of a tower in a business district, one summer afternoon at the end of the twentieth century. After a long meeting, everyone had been drinking coffee in the sunshine of the tower's terrace café. His colleagues had taken off their jackets and loosened their ties; some had even put on sunglasses. Laurent left the group and went over to the steel guard-rail. He looked down at the figures in the square below, preceded at that hour by enormously elongated shadows. Some were moving slowly, others trotting briskly like ants – surely towards a meeting which they must not be late for. The air was burning his skin, the tower blocks bright in the sun and sharp like quartz rising from the earth. He lowered his head towards the 140 metres of emptiness. He thought it would only take a few seconds. His colleagues would be stupefied; some would drop their coffee cups, others would open their mouths wide without emitting any sound. He would leave behind the young woman he had just met, Claire; she would remake her life with someone better than him. Many years later she would remember that sad relationship she had started with the boy who had killed himself without leaving a letter of explanation.

An existence devoted to reading would have been his ultimate fulfilment, but it had not been given to him. He would have had to choose that path much earlier, to have known what he wanted to do straight after the baccalauréat. To have had a life plan. Laurent had let himself be drawn into studying law, which had led to the bank. At first it had been interesting to be recognised as a promising young banker, to climb the hierarchy, to have responsibilities and to earn a lot of money. Up until the day he had started to feel, dimly at first, then more and more clearly, that the man he had become was the absolute opposite of what he really was. Although the dichotomy weighed heavily on him, for a while the money he was earning was compensation enough, but then it could no longer make up for it. The gap between his ideal and his reality was too great. The weight turned into an anguish which was succeeded by the intolerable idea that he was wasting his life – or even that he had already wasted it. Laurent backed away from the railing then turned towards his colleagues. He contemplated them, aware that something momentous had just taken place: he had coldly considered climbing over the railing of an office block at La Défense.

'I'm going to change jobs,' he told Claire that evening – without telling her about the strange impulse that had come over him as he stared into the void. 'I'm going to open a bookshop.'

She had spoken to him for a long time about it, had asked him to think about it carefully. Then she had said nothing more. Laurent had negotiated an amicable departure from the bank. Claire was promoted; the word 'deputy' was no longer appended to her title as marketing director of a frozen food brand. Laurent had bought the commercial lease of the Celtique, and the same week, Claire had announced that she was pregnant. A new life began.

The end of the dream never changed: he climbed over the railing and as the thrill of the fall took hold of him, he woke up. The cat leapt from his lap. The phone in the study was ringing. Laurent rose and went into the room. The answer phone had been activated. A button with a little envelope on it began to flash on the keypad, then stopped. Laurent hesitated then pressed on the envelope.

The loudspeaker said, 'You have one new message. Message

received at 8.46. "Good evening, Laure ... It's Franck. I haven't heard from you; you're not answering your mobile, so ... I know I was awkward last time, but ... well, it's up to you. This will be my last message ... I won't call again if you don't ring me. So that's it." To listen to the message again press one, to save it press two, to delete press three.'

Laurent looked at the machine and pressed three. 'Your message has been deleted. End of messages. To return to the main menu press nine; for other options press two.'

'Hélène … Hélène, look … the line on the monitor's rising. I'll stay with her,' said a female voice.

'Call Doctor Baulieu,' replied another woman's voice. 'Tell him there's movement in the left hand.'

A prickling sensation. Vague at first before she pinned it down. The tips of her fingers and toes. She had gradually become aware of her own body again. She could hear the blood beating more and more loudly in her ears. The vast, sweet universe she had been floating in had shrunk to fit within a single room. Although everything remained dark, she could sense she was in a space enclosed by walls and a ceiling. Her mind could roam around the room; it didn't take long to explore. Wherever she was, it was a quiet place to be lying in. She opened her eyes. Everything looked blurry, too bright and fuzzy, like a camera out of focus. A shadow moved towards her, hazy around the edges as if behind frosted glass.

'Hello,' said the shadow. 'You're waking up.'

The shadow came closer. Its face was still blurred but she was beginning to make out eyes, a nose, a mouth and blonde hair. She had heard this woman's voice before, while she was asleep.

'Don't worry,' she said, 'there's no lasting damage. You're not hurt.'

Her mouth was not moving in time with the words. The sound was a good second behind.

'Everything will look a bit fuzzy,' said the blonde shadow. 'Don't try to talk. Blink twice if you can hear me and understand what I'm saying.'

Laure blinked twice.

'That's great,' said the shadow encouragingly. 'You're coming out of a coma. You've been in hospital for two weeks. Do you understand?'

Laure opened her mouth to reply.

'Sshhh,' said the shadow, putting a finger to Laure's lips as if to stop her spilling a secret.

'Close your eyes,' she said softly, 'and try to take in what I've just told you. Take your time. There's no lasting damage. You're not hurt,' the voice repeated before placing her hand on Laure's. 'I'm right here, I'm not going anywhere. Everything's fine.'

'I'm your doctor,' said the head with white hair, which was a bit less fuzzy than the woman's face. 'Don't try to answer. As the nurse told you, you're doing well. Can you nod your head? That's good. I'm going to ask you a few questions and you can nod like that to answer. Can you see a little more clearly now than when you first woke up? Good. Is there a delay before you hear my voice? Good, that's normal; it'll pass. Wiggle your left foot, very good. Right foot, perfect, your right index finger, no, the index finger, thank you, your left little finger, and again, very good, breathe in, breathe out, perfect. Now we're going to say a sentence: the robin is sitting on the branch. Off you go.'

Laure repeated after him, her voice hoarse.

'What a lovely voice,' commented the doctor.

Laure made a face.

'I'm going to ask four questions that may seem a little strange. Are you ready?'

Laure nodded.

'Can you tell me the name of a cuddly toy or doll you were especially fond of as a little girl?'

'Foxy,' whispered Laure after a pause.

'Good,' said Baulieu. 'Presumably Foxy was a fox?'

Laure nodded.

'Where were you on 11 September 2001?'

'In Kuwait ... gilding ... the palace of Prince Al-Sabah.'

Baulieu shook his head.

'That's a first,' he said. 'Never heard that one before. What's your name?'

'Laure. Laure Valadier.'

'Last question: do you know why you're here?'

'My bag ...' she murmured.

'Don't talk too much,' said William, stroking her hand. 'You mustn't wear yourself out.'

'Thank you for being here. What about Belphégor...?' she asked in a whisper.

'Don't worry, he's fine. Laurent took care of everything.'

'Laurent ... Who's Laurent?'

At the very moment Laure was asking that question – to which William replied with an uneasy silence – Laurent was pushing open the cast-iron gate to three large courtyards that led on from one another. They had both agreed during the 'cat time' phone conversation the previous evening to meet the following day at the workshop so that Laurent could return the keys. As he was looking around for the sign indicating which workshop was where, his gaze was attracted by a paving stone in the courtyard covered in gold. There was another one a few metres away and further on a third one. Like a fairy-tale trail, all you had to do was follow the golden stones to the third courtyard and the glass frontage of the Ateliers Gardhier. A curly-haired woman wearing little gold glasses was smoking a cigarette in front of the door. She wore black jeans and white Repetto pumps. Laurent said hello to her as he entered the building, where he found himself in a vast hallway whose walls were covered in ladders, ropes and tools that he did not recognise.

'Can I help you?' the woman asked him.

'Yes, I have a meeting with William.'

'I'm sorry, he's not here,' she said, blowing her cigarette smoke into the light.

'Oh.' Laurent was disconcerted. 'I was supposed to return Laure's keys to him. Laure Valadier?'

'You're a friend of Laure's?'

'Yes, I was feeding her cat.'

'It's Laure he's gone to see. The hospital called, she's just come round.'

'How is she?'

'I think she's fine, but William didn't go into detail; he left very quickly. He was very anxious. Well, you know what William's like ...' and the woman ended with a rueful smile.

'Good, that's very good,' murmured Laurent. 'Everything is very good,' he added in a low voice as if just to himself, then he smiled back at the woman. 'Could I ask you a favour?' he said, taking the duplicate keys out of his pocket. 'Could you give him Laure's keys?'

'Of course,' she said, stubbing out her cigarette. Laurent handed over the keys, said goodbye and went out into the courtyard, following the golden paving stones. He knew what he had to do: he had to put out of his mind those two extraordinary days and the illusion of being with the woman he must never now meet. How would she accept the fact that a stranger had inveigled himself into her home, had fed her cat and passed himself off as her lover? He himself would have difficulty explaining his actions if by chance anyone should ask him to justify them. To the questions: Why did you personally try to find the owner of the bag? Why did you wait for an author in a park two days in a row? Why did you pay Aphrodite Dry-cleaner's with your own money? Why did you not correct Laure's friend when he took you for her lover? Laurent could only answer truthfully, but unsatisfactorily: I don't know.

'So it appears I let in an imaginary man who fed a real-life cat for two days,' William concluded.

Laure and Baulieu were watching him in silence.

'Have you seen him again since?' Laure asked.

'No,' William replied weakly, laughing nervously at how ridiculous his answer sounded.

'I'm sorry, William, but I don't know any booksellers called Laurent,' Laure said.

'Right, I think we'll leave it there,' said Baulieu. 'I'll be back later this afternoon.'

'And I'll be back tomorrow morning,' added William. 'Get some rest,' he told her, stroking her hand.

'We need to find out who it was, don't we, William? Will you let me know who it was that came to my flat?'

'Yes, my lovely,' he said, planting a kiss on her forehead. 'Don't fret, everything's fine.'

Laure smiled and turned to look at the ventilator beside the next bed. The sound it made was hypnotic, soft and repetitive. Perhaps this was what had inspired the running water in her dream?

William and the doctor went out into the corridor.

'No.' Baulieu stopped him before he even had the chance to ask the question.

'But, doctor, I really think ...'

'No,' Baulieu said again.

'She has no memory of the man she's dating. She must be suffering from amnesia.'

'One more time: no, Laure does not have amnesia. I'm sorry, but we've carried out all the tests. I don't have an explanation, but as far as I'm concerned it's not a medical issue.'

There was a heavy silence. It seemed to William that however 'unique' Baulieu's sense of humour, he was currently displaying none at all. His tone was almost cold, in fact, and he seemed anxious to draw the discussion to a close.

'Call the man and ask him who he is.'

'I don't have his mobile number,' muttered William. 'Or any other way of contacting him.'

The hospital and the Ateliers Gardhier were seventeen Métro stops and a change of line apart. As the stops went by, William came up with a string of ever more outlandish theories: from potential burglar, he was now suspecting Laurent of being some kind of apparition. The criminal hypothesis had gone out the window by the third station. Laurent was dressed very respectably and certainly didn't look as if he was hiding a crowbar inside his coat. He also knew Laure's full name. And not only hers, but the cat's. Plus he knew that Laure had met a famous author and asked him to sign her book. In short, he knew Laure, even if she didn't remember him. Yet Baulieu wouldn't entertain the idea of amnesia. I'm the only one who saw him, William told himself again and again. All attempts at a rational explanation seemed to defy logic.

At the fifth station, he typed the words 'acid flashback' into his iPhone and clicked on a Wikipedia article: 'Term first used as part of a 1965 study carried out by William Forsch, a psychiatrist at Bellevue Psychiatric Hospital in New York. Forsch observed that some users of LSD reported effects reminiscent of those caused by the drug several months after taking it.' William had taken magic mushrooms on three occasions. Following the last of these, four years ago, he had spent the night lying in his bathtub talking to the shower head, which talked back. The pair had enjoyed a philosophical discussion of a rare intensity, spanning such universal themes as death, the afterlife, the possibility of life on other planets and the existence of God. The shower head came up with precise answers to all these questions. The following morning, William had to concede that the intellectual capacities of his bathroom fittings had severely diminished, and the shower head's gifts were now limited to the provision of hot or cold water in classic or massage mode. That episode had marked the end of his experimentation with mind-altering substances. But neither this nor his previous dalliances with drugs had resulted in a man materialising and striking up a conversation. The Wikipedia article alluded to the possibility of short-lived disturbances in the months following a trip, not years afterwards. The theory did not hold water.

As he walked through the tunnels to change trains, he found himself considering a paranormal explanation. Sitting on one of the seats along the edge of the platform, William imagined that Laurent was the ghost of a long-dead former occupant of the flat – after all, the building dated from 1878 – it said so above the door. He had seen a film a bit like that, with Bruce Willis and a little boy who saw dead people. And there was *Ghost*, of course, with Patrick Swayze and Demi Moore, one of the most romantic films ever made, and Patrick Swayze was unbelievably hot in it – even playing a ghost. All he could think of were Hollywood movie plots, imaginary stories dreamt up by screenwriters. Nothing real.

The train pulled in and as it travelled to the next four stops, William toyed with the idea that Laurent could be the physical manifestation of a man travelling in an astral plane – a kind of lama figure – whose body was in a whole other realm, and who intuitively knew everything: the name of the cat and the owner of the apartment, as well as recent events in her life. But the theory was too muddled and Tibetan – and he knew nothing about astral travel or the mental capacities of lamas. At the eleventh station, he recalled a documentary he had watched a few months ago about an early-twentieth-century priest, Padre Pio. Not only had the holy man received Christ's stigmata, but he also possessed the gift of ubiquity, or 'bilocation', as the documentary put it. Padre Pio was said to have been in several places at the same time, and these places were many thousands of kilometres apart. There were eyewitness accounts to back this up. Despite having kept quiet initially, the Church took the unexpected step of declaring the claims to be genuine.

Grappling with such mystical questions in the middle of a Métro carriage planted two spine-tingling words in William's head: guardian angel. After all, it was while he was in the grip of the cat-feeding dilemma, with no one to stand in for him during his trip to Berlin, that the doorbell had rung. The visitor had agreed to feed the cat while he was away, as if that was exactly what he had come up to the fifth floor to do. To help them, him and Laure. As if that had always been his mission.

William was weighing up the probability of an angel making a visit to central Paris when the warning sound signalled the doors were about to close at his stop. He scrambled to his feet and ran onto the platform. No, none of it added up, angels, lamas or phantoms. Besides, he remembered Laurent had been due to come and drop off the keys that morning, which meant someone else might have seen him. That put his mind at ease, and he left his wild thoughts behind him as the escalator returned him to street level.

He had barely crossed the threshold of the ateliers when he bumped into Pierre carrying a heavy gilt picture frame.

'So,' asked Pierre, 'did you see her? How is she?'

'She's doing well, the doctor's happy, she sends her love to everyone, she should be out in four days.'

Pierre shook his head. 'She's had a close shave,' he said.

'Oh, Pierre, did I have any visitors this morning?'

'No, I didn't see anyone.'

William carried on past Agathe, who was stirring her Armenian bole mixture in front of a contemporary sculpture which was to be entirely covered in gold leaf. She turned to stop him.

'So, how is she?'

'She's doing well, she's conscious, the doctor's happy, she sends her love to everyone, she should be out in four days.'

'Phew,' said Agathe.

'Oh, Agathe, did someone call for me this morning?'

'No, not as far as I know.'

François came towards them, his finished pipe still clenched between his teeth.

'So, did you see her?'

'Yes, she's doing well, her doctor's happy, she sends her love, she should be out in four days.'

'That's what I like to hear, my boy,' said François.

'François, did you by any chance notice anyone asking for me this morning?'

'Nope, no one.'

William closed his eyes.

'William!' Sébastien Gardhier called down from the first-floor mezzanine. 'So, did you see her?'

'Yes, she's doing well, she's conscious, the doctor's happy, and should be out in four days.'

'Marvellous. Send her our love, won't you?' he said.

William crossed the workshop and swooped on Jeanne, who was burnishing some gilding with an agate stone.

'Jeanne,' he said with something approaching solemnity. 'Did someone ask to see me this morning?'

'No,' replied Jeanne. 'Why are you looking at me like that? You're being peculiar. Anyway, how's Laure?'

'She's fine, everything's fine. Everything's great. Amandine,' he mumbled, 'where's Amandine?'

'She popped out to buy something. She shouldn't be long.'

He had been pacing around the courtyard on the pretext of needing some fresh air for a good ten minutes when he glimpsed his colleague across the cobbles.

'Amandine!' he shouted, darting towards her.

Amandine froze.

'My God, no,' she said, holding her fist to her mouth as if to hold back the words. 'Please don't tell me Laure's ...' she whispered.

'No, no! Laure's fine, she's conscious, she'll be out soon.'

'What's the matter with you!' cried Amandine. 'You scared the living daylights out of me. I thought she was dead.'

'Sorry,' stammered William. 'I didn't mean to scare you.'

'I'm still shaking,' she went on, looking down at her hands while William went on apologising profusely. 'Oh, a guy came to give you back her keys,' she added crossly, delving into her jacket pocket.

'So?' said Baulieu, walking in without knocking. 'How are we feeling this morning?'

'Better,' replied Laure.

'Good,' said Baulieu.

He sat down beside her and took her blood pressure, pressing the little button on the machine with a steady hand.

'Have you solved the riddle of the mystery man?' he asked without taking his eyes off the screen.

'We think he must be a neighbour,' said Laure.

Baulieu nodded.

'120/50 ... No dizziness? Nausea? Headaches?'

'A little bit, last night.'

'That's normal. Good, I think we'll soon have you gilding again,' he said with a smile.

'Yes, everything will be just the same as before,' murmured Laure, 'except I'll never get my bag back.'

'You can always buy another one ...'

'No, the things inside it were irreplaceable. You can't replace a piece of your life. I realise that must sound over the top, but it feels that way to me.'

Baulieu smiled in acceptance.

'I believe you,' he said, placing his hand on Laure's. 'You're my last patient. Your waking up is a good note to end my career on.'

'Thank you, Professor,' whispered Laure after a pause.

'No,' said the doctor softly, turning his head towards the window, 'I'm the one who should be thanking you. Do great things, Laure, be happy, or at least do your best to be. Life is fragile; you've found that out for yourself.'

He stood up and smiled at her.

'Just one thing,' he added, rolling up the cuff of his blood-pressure monitor. 'Miserable old cynic that I am, I don't really buy the idea of a neighbour coming in to feed a stranger's cat.'

He winked and left without another word.

Laurent sat at the desk by the entrance checking stock on the computer while, perched on the tall ladder, Maryse tidied up the history shelves. Damien was deep in conversation with one of their favourite customers, Monsieur Belier, a retired École Normale Supérieure maths professor. It was always entertaining to see this formally attired man in matching tie and handkerchief and the tall, long-haired youth with his earring and goatee (whom you might imagine at first glance to be an expert on reggae albums rather than philosophical essays) locked in heated debate. For a good half-hour their conversation provided background noise that was rather agreeable. From the snippets Laurent overheard, the two were arguing amicably about the concept of reality, invoking Descartes and the recent work of mathematician Misha Gromov. For Monsieur Belier, reality did not truly exist, it was formed on our retina from a mixture of emptiness and atoms.

'It exists and at the same time it doesn't exist,' objected Damien.

Laurent turned to look at Maryse who rolled her eyes, indicating that all these concepts were over her head and that was fine with her.

A man of about fifty came through the door and went up to Laurent. 'Do you have *La Nostalgie du Possible*?'

'Yes.' Laurent stared hard at the man, who gave him an embarrassed smile.

'Sorry,' said Laurent. 'I'll go and get it for you.'

Antonio Tabucchi's text on Pessoa. But it wasn't the title that he had heard but an actual question, 'Are you nostalgic for what could have been?' posed by a stranger. A question he had answered truthfully: 'Yes.' And when this random customer had departed with his book, Laurent wondered whether the man had come in purely to put into words the feeling he was living with.

Can you experience nostalgia for something that hasn't happened? We talk of 'regrets' about the course of our lives, when we are almost certain we have taken the wrong decision; but one can also be enveloped in a sweet and mysterious euphoria, a sort of nostalgia for what might have been. Meeting Laure, that might have happened but didn't and yet Laurent remembered the café where they had arranged to meet. She wore that white strappy dress, her mauve bag and sunglasses. It had been a very sunny day. As it was fine they had chosen to sit on the terrace.

'Is it really you, Laurent?' She sat down and removed her sunglasses.

They had looked at each other for a long time, unsure what to say first, then Laure's light-coloured eyes crinkled and she smiled. They talked for ages then went for a walk. Laurent could picture very clearly the way he had walked alongside her down the tree-lined streets. The sun shone through the branches, casting flecks of light onto the road. Laure wore white ballet pumps which passed from shadow into light in time with her steps. Then the pumps had stopped moving. Laurent looked up at her. Laure held his gaze a little too steadily and he had known it was the moment they would kiss.

That was exactly what Tabucchi was suggesting in his title – that we can pass right by something very important: love, a job, moving to another city or another country. Or another life. 'Pass by' and at the same time be 'so close' that sometimes, while in that state of melancholy that is akin to hypnosis, we can, in spite of everything, manage to grab little fragments of what might have been. Like catching snatches of a far-off radio frequency. The message is obscure, yet by listening carefully you can still catch snippets of the soundtrack of the life that never was. You hear sentences that were never actually said, you hear footsteps echoing in places you've never been to, you can make out the surf on a beach whose sand you have never touched. You hear the laughter and loving words of a woman though nothing ever happened between you. The idea of an affair with her had crossed your mind. Perhaps she would have liked that – probably in fact – but nothing ever happened. For some unknown reason, we never gave in to the exquisite vertigo that you feel when you move those few centimetres towards the face of the other for the first kiss. We passed by, we passed so close that something of the experience remains.

Damien and the professor were still debating and were now airing their opinions on the plurality of the universe, quoting from the hypotheses of researchers with Russian-sounding names. Laurent wondered if there were booksellers in these other universes, who also had to heft boxes, take stock, and what's more, find handbags. At that thought he leant back in his chair and looked out at the square. The reality he saw there was perhaps only a mathematical formula in his mind's eye, since his eye did not take in the railings, the trees or the statue. His spirit was elsewhere. At Laure's. On her landing to be precise, advancing towards her door, turning the key in the lock. And there was Belphégor who had immediately come out on the landing to roll around. Laurent entered the apartment and saw the little paintings, the dish with the golden keys, the weeping fig in the light from the window … He went on into the kitchen, poured himself a Jack Daniel's and went through to the sitting room where Laure, seated on the sofa, turned to smile at him.

When they reached her door, William handed her the spare keys and cleared his throat.

'Before you go in, there's something I need to tell you ... I lied to you because I didn't want to upset you.'

Laure's gaze darted towards him.

'Has something happened to my cat?'

'No, no,' said William.

He had been making a real mess of things lately. First he had inadvertently made it sound as if Laure was dead, and now the cat. He took a moment to tell himself he needed a holiday. Thailand, maybe, or Bali. Anywhere, so long as it was far away.

'Your cat's fine. Everything's fine,' he said emphatically.

There was a pause.

'It's about your bag ... it's here, it's back.'

'What?' asked Laure, then, since William didn't respond, she turned the key in the door and Belphégor came running out.

'Oh, my treasure, I'm home!' she cried.

She scooped the cat up in her arms and carried him into the apartment. As soon as she stepped inside the door, she was hit by that feeling of coming home after a long time away, when the dust seems to have been blown off things you had become so used to looking at you had stopped seeing them. Everything suddenly seems more intense, like a photograph restored to its original colour and contrast.

Sunlight was pouring into the living room and the cat leapt from his mistress's arms to roll on the parquet floor. Laure turned to William.

'In your room …' he said.

She made her way to the bedroom door and pushed it open. The bag was sitting on top of the white bed cover and her strappy dress had been laid out on a hanger beside it. Propped against the mauve leather handles, there was an envelope addressed by hand in black fountain pen: For Laure Valadier. William shut his eyes and bit his bottom lip.

After Laurent had returned the keys, William had gone back to the flat that same evening to feed the cat. As he turned the key, he noticed something different: the door had not been double-locked, only pulled shut. He sensed something was up and yet everything else seemed so normal that it was several minutes before he went into the bedroom and found the bag, the dress and the letter. Of course he could not resist the temptation to read it. He had played a part in the events leading up to the reappearance of the bag on the bed, after all. He took the shade off the living-room lamp and held the sealed envelope over the bulb in order to read through the paper.

Laurent the bookseller was not Laure's latest squeeze after all. He was simply a passer-by who had chanced upon the mauve bag in the street. William sat down on the sofa and took the decision not to tell Laure for fear of unsettling her. She was lying in a hospital bed having just come out of a coma. Leading her to believe that the stranger was a do-gooding neighbour seemed the best option in the short term. And it worked.

As soon as he returned to the ward, she bombarded him with questions: Who was this bookseller called Laurent who had come to her flat to look after the cat? How did she know him?

What did he look like? What had he said? William stripped his account of Laurent's arrival down to the bare minimum: he had come to the door asking to speak to Laure. He was very polite. William told him Laure was not at home but in hospital, adding that he had to go away for two days and didn't know who was going to feed the cat. Laurent had kindly volunteered to step in, and William had seen no reason to turn him down. Having laid the groundwork, he could claim with some confidence, 'He's one of your neighbours, Laure. Who else could it be?'

'Yes ...' she eventually conceded, 'you must be right. A few new people have moved into the building. There's a guy on the second floor who seems really nice – it sounds like it could have been him. I thought he was something to do with graphic novels.'

'That's it, then,' William agreed. 'He must run a bookshop that specialises in comics.'

At the time, he had breathed an internal sigh of relief. But not now. It was time to own up: he had left the keys to Laure's flat and the care of her treasured pet in the hands of a complete stranger. Now Laure was sitting on the edge of the bed, she had opened the envelope and was reading the short letter that William knew by heart.

Dear Laure Valadier,

I'm sorry to have intruded so far into your life. It wasn't my intention. I found your bag one morning in the street, and got caught up in trying to find the owner so that I could return it. Things then ran a little out of control.

I now know that you are recovered. I know also that I have given up on the idea of meeting you. I went too far. To quote Patrick Modiano, whom you seem to like, in Villa Triste, *'There are mysterious beings, always the same, who watch over us at each crossroads in our lives.' Let's just say that, unintentionally, I have been one of those beings.*

Best wishes

Laurent

The objects lay scattered silently over the bed. The cat had jumped onto the covers and was sniffing each item carefully. Everything she had grieved for and believed lost for ever had just reappeared.

The first thing she had touched as she felt inside the bag was the brass compact mirror with birds on, given to her by her grandmother on her eighth birthday. 'It's about time this mirror reflected a pretty young girl's face again,' she had joked. It was the first 'beautiful' gift Laure had ever received, and she had carried it with her ever since.

Next came her keys and the Egyptian pendant bearing her name, a reward for her work in Cairo. The chain it originally hung on had broken six months earlier and she had fixed it to her key ring instead, using a pair of jeweller's pliers borrowed from the Ateliers Gardhier. Her fingers brushed the guilloche ornamentation on her mother's gold cigarette lighter which she kept in her bag in case friends who smoked needed a light. She took it out and rolled the wheel; it produced a flame.

Right at the bottom of the bag, she found the three pebbles: the small white one she and Xavier had picked up on Antìparos in the Cyclades in 2002; the long grey one collected on a walk in a park in Edinburgh four years ago; and the round black one from Brittany or the Midi, she couldn't remember which ... Her diary was there, along with Xavier's Montblanc pen. The hair clip with the blue fabric flower she had owned since she was fifteen, having coveted it in the shop window for weeks. The plastic had never broken, proof that the accessories on offer at Candice Beauté must be of the highest order. Her lucky pair of red craps dice bought in London five years ago in a specialist games shop, which she sometimes used to help her make decisions. Her Chanel Coco Shine lipstick in a corally shade of red; the *ris de veau* recipe she had torn out of *Elle* at the dentist's two weeks ago, just as he walked in – he must have seen her do it but said nothing. *Accident Nocturne* by Patrick Modiano, which she opened on the flyleaf. *Excuse me ... I'm sorry to come up to you in the street like this; I don't normally do this kind of thing, honestly, but ... You're Patrick Modiano, aren't you? ... Yes ... Well ... Yes, I ... I am.*

No mobile phone, just the charger. No purse either, but the red Moleskine notebook was there. Laure opened it and read over her own thoughts, scribbled down on Métro journeys or while sitting on café terraces. The lists of things she liked or was scared of. A reminder to buy food for Belphégor. A dream, another dream. Then she pulled out the envelope with the photos and found the picture of her parents taken on a road in the Midi sometime in the late 1970s, and the one of Xavier standing in her parents' garden by the apple tree. She had taken it just before one of those summer lunches she had revisited in her dreams that week. The third picture was of the house, taken from the bottom of the garden; if you looked carefully, you could spot Sarbacane hiding up in the weeping willow.

Laure reached for Belphégor, closing her eyes and running her fingers through his fur. She had thought she would never see these pictures again, having kept them safe in her bag for years; the negatives were long since lost. The receipt from the dry-cleaner's was no longer inside the little pocket, but the dress was there, spotless in its plastic wrapping. She took a hairgrip out of her bag and pinned back the strands falling into her face. Next to her make-up bag and the Modiano she placed the half-full bottle of Evian she had sipped from in the taxi minutes before the mugging. The bag seemed to contain even more than she remembered, and as she took out forgotten belongings, she felt like a child sitting under the Christmas tree, unwrapping the gifts from her red cotton stocking. Her sister had had the same stocking and the exact same number of presents, but always finished opening them more quickly so that she could claim Laure had more than her. She sprayed her wrist with perfume, brought it slowly to her nose and closed her eyes.

'William ...' she said.

Frozen in the doorway, William replied with a faint 'Yes?'

'Tell me about this Laurent.'

I like the way this man has slipped away without leaving an address.
  I like his letter.
  I like the fact that he works in a bookshop.
  I'm scared he might be a bit nuts.
  I'm scared I'll never meet him.

I find the idea of a stranger coming into my flat terrifying, but I like the idea that Belphégor wasn't scared of him. Which proves the man is not terrifying (paradox).

I like the idea of a man going to so much trouble to find me (no one has ever gone to so much trouble for me before).

How many booksellers in Paris are called Laurent?

She was almost certain she had not lit a fire, but she could not have sworn to it. Perhaps he had burnt a few logs one night when it was chilly, perhaps not. Apart from this one detail, there was no trace of Laurent in the flat. The man had passed in and out again like a draught. The only one who could remember him being there was the cat, who had watched him coming and going but refused to say a word about it. Laurent, as this man was called, must have let his eyes wander over her things, the paintings on the walls, and certainly the books on the shelves. Given what he did for a living, might her reading tastes have played a hand in convincing him to carry on his search? Had his interest been piqued by her signed copy of *Accident Nocturne*, making him want to know more about the person who had mustered the courage to stop Patrick Modiano in the street?

It was late, and by now Laure knew Laurent's letter off by heart. He had apparently found her bag in the street – but which street? He had probably taken it home with him and emptied out its contents, examining each item like a detective looking for clues. He must be slightly crazy. Or very romantic. Or have too much time on his hands. Or a bit of all three, Laure thought. He had combed through her diary and, what was more, her red Moleskine notebook. That meant he knew everything she liked or was afraid of, even the contents of her dreams. None of her lovers had ever known as much about her. Only Xavier had been allowed to hear a few of her lists of 'likes' and 'fears', and even then Laure had filtered them carefully. Never before nor after Xavier had she allowed any man to know what lay between those pages. She had lost count of the number of notebooks she had filled since adolescence. They were all carefully stored inside four shoe boxes in the cellar.

And now there was a man in the city who knew almost all there was to know about her. A man whom she had never met yet who was familiar with the decor of her home, had studied her belongings at leisure and stroked her cat, knew exactly what was inside her bag, what she liked to read, what her bedroom looked like. Other men besides Xavier had been allowed access to her body, but no one else had really stepped inside her mind. It was not for want of trying: Laure simply refused to open up. It was more than she was capable of.

Franck, the man she had most recently been seeing, had discovered this to his cost. He had insisted on coming back to her place. As soon as he walked in, Belphégor scurried under the sofa. Franck took it upon himself to pass judgement on Laure's belongings. The collection of dice in the study struck him as 'bizarre'. As soon as he left the room, Laure took the opportunity to throw a pair – she got a one and a two. 'You've got Sophie Calle's books? Bit bonkers, that woman, isn't she?' Laure said nothing. As the minutes ticked by, she could feel herself stiffen. She knew she had to be mindful of her pale eyes narrowing wolf-like in anger. When he made a comment about William, expounding what he thought was a very clever theory about 'gay best friends' seeing their female friends as substitute sisters or mothers, Laure knew she would not be sleeping with him that night. Besides, Franck was a pretty average lover. She played the sudden headache card and sent him home. The cat came back out from under the sofa, visibly furious at having had to spend over an hour under there, and took himself off to bed without deigning to look at his mistress.

To search for a woman using her stolen handbag for clues. None of the men she had known would ever have embarked on such an enterprise. Not her father, not Xavier. That said ... she was sure Xavier would have taken the things out of a discarded handbag and looked at them, but would he have managed to track down their owner without ID or a phone? Just how had Laurent managed to trace her all the way back to her apartment, in fact? William said he had heard the bell, opened the door and found him standing on the landing. Laure was certain that nothing in her bag – apart from the purse – had her name on, still less her address. He said he had tried to phone several times – yes, her number was in the phone book, but he would have had to know her name to find it. All he had to go on was the Modiano book with the dedication inside. And that would only have provided her Christian name. Even using the patience and skills of deduction of a first-rate detective, he still wouldn't have known her surname. He had gone so far as to pick up her strappy dress from the dry-cleaner's, no doubt by matching the date in the diary with the one on the receipt – well observed, but no one at Aphrodite Dry-cleaner's knew her surname or where she lived.

Come to think of it, I don't know any more about him than he knew about me at the beginning: I've got nothing but a Christian name to go on, mused Laure as she got into the bubble bath she had run herself. The cat leapt up onto the side of the tub and posed statue-like in one corner, without taking his eyes off her.

'You saw him, you know all about him. Tell me something,' she pleaded.

The cat narrowed his golden eyes and stared at his mistress. Laure was reminded of the Egyptian goddess Bastet – Belphégor had adopted exactly the same pose. She closed her eyes. She had dreamt of this moment over the last few days in hospital, telling herself that as soon as she slipped under the orange-blossom bubbles, it would all be over. The scorching-hot water and foam surrounded her breasts and then her neck as she let her head slide down the tub until her ears went underwater. All outside noise was muffled and she found herself enveloped in warm, cocoon-like silence. Out of habit, she slipped her hand between her breasts but there was nothing there. Since the gold chain had snapped, she no longer wore anything around her neck. The little red enamel Fabergé egg pendant inherited from her mother was now safely stowed in a bedroom drawer. As for the Egyptian cartouche, she had attached it to her key ring.

Laure opened her eyes and pulled herself upright. The cartouche with the hieroglyphics. That was the one object that bore her surname.

Chloé looked at her father; he seemed to be put out and absent. He could not stop looking at the shelf of cat food, particularly the display of five blue packets of Virbac – 'Adult cat – *au canard*, with duck'. Claire wasn't in Paris, and Bertrand was at a photographic shoot. Laurent had been called in to help with Putin's annual visit to the vet. The cat was on Chloé's lap in his basket, giving intermittent little growls that Chloé immediately silenced by running her fingers along the wire. Perhaps she had been harsh when she told him the other night that he had been an idiot to terminate the bag saga in that way. She had been so disappointed that the whole beautiful search which she had participated in a little had ended with a letter to which Laure would not be able to respond. Laurent had been immovable. No, he shouldn't have put his telephone number or email address at the end of the letter. He had to disappear, and cover his traces; on no account did he want to find himself having to answer the quite legitimate questions that the owner of the handbag would have for him. Perhaps it was excessive masculine caution. Or a misunderstanding of feminine psyche and its needs? Laurent had taken a route that not only offered an elegant solution but had also closed down the affair for ever.

'Was there a cat over there too?' said Chloé. It was as if she was referring to a far-off land where he would never go again, like those exiles who recall the land of their birth.

'Yes,' said Laurent seriously.

'What was he like?'

'Black.'

'And what was the name again?'

'Belphégor,' replied Laurent.

'Not the cat's, hers.'

'Valadier.'

'Putin,' said the vet loudly, coming into the waiting room.

Two ladies with little dogs looked up from their magazines and exchanged glances. One of them raised her eyebrows in consternation; the other shook her head.

'Poor cat,' one murmured.

As soon as he was out of the basket, Putin looked fierce and hissed at the vet.

'He's always so happy to see me,' commented the vet, trying to sound jolly. 'He's a great advertisement for our profession, your cat.'

Laurent was looking at photos of animals pinned on the wall. Between a husky and a Norwegian cat, there was a black cat, still as a statue, staring into the lens and apparently waiting patiently.

Laure took a seat outside a café and ordered a noisette. Had she been a smoker, now would have been the moment to light up with that air of concentration adopted by all nicotine consumers as they take their first drag. Twelve bookshops, and not a single Laurent matching his description. She went back to her notes of William's account: fairly tall, slim, light-brown hair, mid-forties, brown eyes.

The previous evening, she had made a list of all the local bookshops, immediately striking off L'Île en Livre and Fleur de Mots where she bought books regularly and knew all the staff either by name or sight. She was working on the basis that the thief had probably not crossed the whole of Paris to dump her bag, and therefore there was a strong possibility Laurent worked in the immediate area, or at least within the same arrondissement. The waiter brought Laure her coffee and she poured in a sachet of sugar. She had started with Au Fil des Pages, a bookshop five streets from where she lived.

'Hello, bit of a strange question, but do you by any chance have a bookseller called Laurent working here?'

Laure had asked the same thing no less than eight times, softly and with an apologetic smile. In the end she met a total of four different Laurents. The first time the blonde girl answered, 'Yes, of course, I'll just call him down,' she felt her stomach flip. The girl came out from behind the till and disappeared between the shelves.

'Laurent,' she called up the stairs. 'There's someone here to see you.'

'He's coming,' she told Laure on her return, before moving on to serve the next customer.

A man in his forties with light-brown hair and little steel-rimmed glasses came down to greet her.

'Hello, great to meet you at last!' he exclaimed, holding out his hand. 'Did you find it OK?'

Laure went quiet for a moment, feeling a little flustered. Then, holding his gaze, she smiled and told him actually it had not been plain sailing.

'Tell me about it,' he agreed, sounding exasperated. 'Since they started the roadworks in the middle of the crossing it's become much harder to spot us, but you got here, that's the main thing. I'll show you where the paperbacks are,' he said, motioning for her to follow him. 'You have to keep a close eye on them because these are the ones that get nicked, but you know all that. Your other section is just on the table here and on these five shelves: crime. You said in your email you were very familiar with American crime writers, which is great, but I'm keen on French detective novels too. What have you read recently?'

Laure stared back at him.

'You must have the wrong person,' she said, smiling in confusion.

'*The Wrong Person?*' asked the bookseller, frowning. 'No, I don't think we do have that one. Who's the author?'

The poor man didn't have a clue about the business of the bag and the cat and Laure backed out of the shop, muttering her apologies. There were no booksellers by the name of Laurent at L'Enjolivre, and none at La Compagnie des Mots, L'Arbre à Mots or La Belle Plume either. The owner of Le Chat à Lunettes, on the other hand, smiled broadly at Laure's question.

'Laurent …? That's me.'

The only thing was he was in his sixties, with white hair and glasses with sky-blue plastic frames. Laure found herself giving another garbled account of how her bag had been returned to her by a bookseller called Laurent, who had fed her cat but left no address for her to contact him.

'I'm sorry, I don't think I'm being very clear,' said Laure, making a mental note to leave out the bit about the cat from now on, because it was all getting way too difficult to explain to a complete stranger who had no idea what she was going on about.

'No, no, it's perfectly clear to me. I can think of far more complicated stories about bags and cats,' the bookseller replied. 'Take this one, for example. Listen carefully: On my way to Notre-Dame, I see a man with seven wives. Seven wives each with seven bags. And in each of those seven bags, seven cats. Seven cats with seven kittens each. How many are going to Notre-Dame?'

'… Forty-nine times forty-nine, plus seven women, plus the man … A lot,' replied Laure.

'No,' said the bookseller, 'not a lot. The answer is one. I'm the only one going to Notre-Dame; as for the man, the women, the bags and cats, we'll never know. You lose, but don't worry, no one ever gets it right. Lunch?'

Laure politely declined the offer from 'the cat with glasses' and went on with her search. She encountered another two Laurents on her way: a tall, dark man with close-cropped hair and a short man with a greying beard. As she neared the end of her list, she made do with opening the door and glancing around the shop floor. None of the staff at these bookshops matched the description William had given. The three at L'Arc en Mots were all women, and there was only a blonde woman sitting behind the till and a tall boy with a goatee at Le Cahier Rouge. La Boîte à Livres was run by a pair of men, but neither fitted the bill. She was about to stake her bet on Mots Passants, where a man in his forties with light-brown hair was bending down to look at a computer screen, when the telephone by his side began to ring. He picked it up.

'Good afternoon, Mots Passants,' he said, before immediately adding, 'No, it's Pierre ...'

Even if Laurent had found the bag around here, his bookshop was not necessarily nearby. He might very well live in this arrondissement and own a bookshop on the opposite side of town. It was also perfectly conceivable that he had only been passing through the area. The thief could have driven off after the mugging, perhaps jumping on a scooter parked a few streets away. He might even have taken the Métro and dumped her bag ten stops away. She wondered what Sophie Calle would have done with a story like hers. Something infinitely more poetic than the afternoon she had just endured, that was for sure.

Laure slowly resigned herself to the idea that the game was up, the trail had gone cold and she would never meet the stranger who had quoted Modiano, fed her cat and written: 'I'm sorry to have intruded so far into your life. It wasn't my intention.' She placed her mauve bag on her lap, took out the purse she had bought the day before and picked out the correct change. Returning it to the bag, her fingers brushed against her lucky red dice. Will I meet Laurent the bookseller one day? she asked silently, and then she dropped the two dice onto the white marble table. A wry smile crossed her lips. If fate was optimistic, as the numbers suggested, the reality was anything but. She picked up her Montblanc pen and one by one crossed out the names of the twelve bookshops in her red notebook.

In the large glass-fronted office on the first floor, Chloé looked at the director of the Ateliers Gardhier in silence.

'It's an eighteenth-century frame, typical of its time. The gold is very faded,' murmured Sébastien Gardhier, inspecting the frame of the little still life. 'You'll have to come back in a month. I hope your parents are not in too much of a hurry?'

Chloé shook her head. 'Can I go and see the people working in your studio?'

Sébastien smiled at her. 'Yes, you can. You can also ask them some questions, but above all you must watch closely. That's the first thing: you have to look,' he said, raising his index finger. 'So off you go and keep your eyes open,' he added, walking her over to the stairs.

'It's horrible, that frame,' she had said the previous evening at dinner.

Bertrand followed her gaze as far as the little picture on the wall. 'Don't say that, Chloé,' he replied, cut to the quick. 'That picture means a lot to me, it comes from my father.'

'It's not the picture that's horrible,' Chloé murmured, 'it's the frame. Look, it's all tarnished.'

'That's true,' Betrand conceded. 'It certainly wasn't always like that.'

The picture was of a lobster in the middle of a fine still life. Chloé explained that the mother of one of her school friends was a gilder; perhaps she could take it to her?

'The picture isn't a priority,' said Claire evasively.

'Now it is,' cut in Bertrand portentously. 'I'm delighted that Chloé is taking an interest in one of my possessions. Tomorrow morning, Chloé, you can take it down, we'll wrap it up together and you can take it to your friend.'

'It might be expensive,' said Chloé in a little voice, pretending to get out of it.

'That doesn't matter,' said Bertrand, still in that tone that brooked no refusal. 'I can easily afford to have that frame gilded.'

Chloé nodded then announced she was going to get the dessert from the kitchen.

Claire looked at Bertrand. 'I appreciate you doing that,' she said softly. 'Thank you.'

'You know,' said Bertrand, helping himself to some wine, 'underneath her rebellious façade, I think your daughter has the makings of a real little homemaker. She's going to surprise us.'

A first name, surname and profession. It had only taken Chloé four minutes to find Laure Valadier's work address.

In the silent studio seven gilders were at work. The first one she came across was a young man with bleached, shaved hair. She quickly eliminated the men: him, the bearded one with grey hair chewing his unlit pipe, and the short one with gelled hair. A dark-haired woman with a ponytail turned to her and smiled.

'I'm allowed to watch,' said Chloé quietly, walking towards her.

The woman was laying gold leaves next to each other on a large glass sheet. The movement of the brush from cheek to the gilding cushion was strangely hypnotic. Each leaf was placed to the millimetre in the correct position. Chloé looked at the woman. Even though she was pretty, something told Chloé that her father would not fall in love with a woman like this. And she immediately dismissed the next woman along who had short blonde hair and a pinched expression. Definitely not, thought Chloé. The one with curly hair and little gold glasses, might she read Modiano, stop him in the street to ask him to sign a book and put it away in a mauve handbag? Chloé went over to her. She looked good in her faded jeans and white Repetto pumps. Was this Laure? The woman looked up and Chloé smiled at her. She didn't know what to think. Her lipstick was pearly pink, and she wore sea-green eyeliner. Chloé hadn't seen anything in the make-up bag that would suit this woman.

She took a step sideways behind a panel covered in gold leaf and found herself looking at a woman with light-coloured eyes. Pale blue or grey. She went over to her. She had shoulder-length brown hair pulled up on top with a blue flower hair clip turned between three twists of hair. She was wearing a grey sweater, a slim-fitting black skirt and high-heeled ankle boots. As Chloé approached, she noted the lovely complexion, and a little detail – she had a beauty spot above her upper lip. She was applying her gold leaves to the base of an antique statue with that movement which made the gold leaf crinkle with static electricity and then smoothing it onto the damp surface. She took a knife and on her calfskin gilding cushion trimmed the next leaf into a triangle, then placed it at an angle and pressed it with precision into the base. 'Hello,' she said softly. 'You're having a look around our studio?'

'Yes, I brought in a frame for my parents and I wanted to see how you worked.'

'Good idea. You see how we all have our leather gilding cushion and knife; there are twelve steps to go through before you get to what I am doing.' She then went on in a friendly manner, 'In fact, you can gild almost anything.' She smiled and her eyes lit up. 'I've done plenty of things, ceilings, railings, roofs ...'

But Chloé wasn't listening any more, she was staring at the cashmere jumper on which she had just spotted a characteristic little shining point caught in the fibres and resistant to any fluff remover: a cat hair. Black. There was another, and another. She leant close to Laure and closed her eyes: yes, definitely Habanita. There was no doubt, here she was, the woman with the mauve handbag. Chloé opened her eyes just as Laure was preparing to place a new leaf.

'His name is Laurent Letellier,' she murmured. 'He's the owner of Le Cahier Rouge.'

Laure's hand stopped in mid-air, the gold leaf lost its static and fell twisting to the ground.

Wednesday 12 February

I haven't kept a diary since I was seventeen. I think it was soon after my baccalauréat that I gave it up for reasons I'm not sure of, because from the age of twelve or thirteen I had written one religiously. (Note to self: Look for my diaries in the boxes in the cellar.) I remember sticking all kinds of things in them: tickets from films and plays I had been to see, leaves I had picked up on walks and bills for meals I had eaten on café terraces. They were a record of what I had done when, down to the nearest minute. I think I held on to them as 'evidence' of some kind. They helped me to find my place in the world and, in a broader sense, to prove to myself that I really existed. I suppose I must have decided at some point that I no longer needed to do that, because I gave up writing a diary, stopped telling the story of my life and tried to just live it instead.

I'm certainly not planning to go back to writing down everything I do each day. For starters, I don't do enough noteworthy things, and besides I already jot stuff in my red notebook if the urge takes me. But since this morning, I've been feeling the need to make a record of what has happened. I know the name and address of the man who brought my bag back. His name is Laurent Letellier. He's the owner of Le Cahier Rouge. I've just realised that's almost word for word what his daughter told me. That sentence was so unexpected and it's still lingering in my mind, bouncing around inside my head like that ancient video game with two lines either side of the screen and a dot going back and forth between them. I once spent an entire Saturday playing it with Natacha Rosen and her brother, David. That was over thirty years ago. I don't know what they're doing now, but I'm pretty sure I'm the only one of us currently thinking about that rainy Saturday at their house in Garches.

The bookseller's daughter is called Chloé. I had coffee with her sitting by the window of the studio. My grandmother would have described her as 'a very determined little person'. That's exactly what she is.

'I think my dad wishes he'd given you his address, and I think you'd like to have it,' she said without beating around the bush. She knows the whole story. I told her I had done the rounds of all the local bookshops, and she seemed to like that idea.

'I'd have done exactly the same thing,' she remarked, running her hand through her hair in a very feminine and ever so slightly arrogant way (was I like that at her age?). I had actually been into her father's bookshop, but I hadn't asked if there was a bookseller called Laurent. I'd had enough of the endless curious looks and disappointments by then.

'When did you go to Le Cahier?' she asked. She took out a Pléiade diary, telling me her father gave her one every year and she could get me one too if I wanted. Then she said something I had to get her to repeat: 'Thursday? That's the day we took Putin to get his jabs.' (Chloé has a cat called Putin – she wouldn't tell me why.) After that she stood up, saying it was time to go to school. She asked me to promise never to tell her father she had come. I promised.

She also asked if I had a husband and children. I told her I didn't have children, but that I had had a husband and that he was dead, that he had been killed a long way away in Baghdad in a terrorist attack. Chloé looked straight at me, shaking her head very slowly without saying a word. I liked the fact she held my gaze; normally when I tell people, they look away and then turn back with sympathy in their eyes, and I feel like giving them a slap.

Thursday 13 February

I pressed the buzzer and heard his voice. It was a little after 8 p.m. The bookshop shutters were down. There were a number of names on the building's intercom, including a certain 'L. Letellier'.

'Hello?' said the voice.

I wanted to reply: 'I'm Laure Valadier ... ' He would probably have paused for a moment and told me to come up. Or perhaps he would have come down. But I couldn't get the words out. I suddenly felt the need to give myself a bit more time, so I said, 'I'm sorry, I've got the wrong address.'

'No problem. Have a good evening,' the voice replied, and the conversation ended with a click.

I remained outside the glass door, looking in at the entrance hall. There was a door on the right which must be the way into the bookshop; the same kind of door leads to the design shop Arcane 17 beneath my flat. I looked at the staircase and the mosaic tiled floor, and thought about the fact that these were things this man – whom I don't know but who knows me so well – saw every day. Chloé told me he has not always been a bookseller; he used to be an investment banker until one day he decided to pack it all in. As someone who has been doing the same thing for the last twenty-four years, I like the idea that it's possible to start a new life.

As I walked back to the taxi rank, I kept thinking how strange it was that we had actually spoken, although he didn't know it. Even distorted by the intercom, he had a nice voice, and his 'Have a good evening' stayed with me throughout my dinner at Jacques and Sophie's. Everywhere I go I end up having to tell the whole story of the mugging and the coma; I'm getting a bit tired of talking about it. I haven't even mentioned it to my sister, who sent me an email saying, 'No news? All good?' I replied, 'Yes, all good, you?' I'm not sure I ever will tell her everything that's happened over the last two weeks. I have less and less in common with Bénédicte and when we talk about the past, our memories are completely at odds. Sometimes it feels as if we didn't have the same parents.

*

Friday 14 February

Today I imitated Sophie Calle. I went to see the bookshop from the outside. I found a bench in the square and sat looking through the window of Le Cahier Rouge. There were three people inside: a tall boy with a goatee and long hair, a blonde woman in her sixties, and Laurent. He is much as William described him. (William, by the way, can't get over the fact I've found his address – he keeps badgering me to go into the shop.) Laurent is indeed 'fairly tall, slim, light-brown hair, mid-forties, brown eyes', but then I always knew William could be relied upon to describe a guy. At first I had to watch him from a distance because I didn't want to get too close to the shop window. I know he would recognise my face. At eleven o'clock, the long-haired bookseller with the goatee came out into the square to meet a guy in a hoodie who sold him some weed. I'm sure that's what it was: a quick, no-nonsense transaction under the statue. I don't know if Laurent is aware of his employee's predilection for marijuana, but the blonde woman gave the kid a look and shook her head in resignation when he came back in – she's definitely on to him.

At lunchtime, Laurent went out, and I followed him. He walked up to the top of Rue de la Pentille and then turned into Rue du Passe-Musette. I was quite a long way behind him and could only see him from the back. It occurred to me I should have brought Xavier's Nikon 51, the only one of his cameras I've ever known how to use. I could have taken pictures and emailed them to him at the bookshop anonymously. He sat down outside a café by the market called l'Espérance. I waited at the corner of the road for a little while before going to sit two tables behind him. The waiter joked that it was quite an event to see him there for lunch. They had a short conversation from which I gathered that Laurent usually visited the café first thing in the morning. I ordered a Caesar salad and a glass of white wine; the bill's pasted below. So it was 1.38 p.m. and the waiter was named on the slip as: garçon 2. Caesar salad: €9.30. Glass of wine: €4.20. Coffee: €2.20. Total: €15.70.

Laurent had a meat dish with a sauce, a glass of red wine and coffee. He spent his lunch break reading a book with a strange-looking white cover. It must have been one of those copies that booksellers get sent before they are published. He had a pencil in his hand and was underlining parts of the text. Leaning forward, I was able to see him in profile. Laurent has a very straight nose and full lips and he hadn't shaved. He has gentle, almost sad-looking eyes which suddenly wrinkled up with laughter when the waiter made some joke I didn't catch. I've always liked men who can go from looking serious to warm in the space of a few seconds. That was true of Xavier, and my father.

Two tables from Laurent there was a blonde woman in a grey suit reading a file. Twice she glanced up at him, drawing on her Vogue cigarette as if deep in thought. She looked like the kind of woman who knew she only had to smile to catch a man's attention, reeling him in in the time it took to ask him to pass the salt.

'I have no sugar,' she said loudly. 'Could I have some sugar please, garçon?'

Laurent, who hadn't used his sugar, didn't even look up from his book while the waiter moved the bowl to the woman's table. Better luck next time, I thought, smiling to myself. As with most men who are attractive without being conventionally handsome, Laurent is clearly oblivious of his charms. The woman left without adding a grain of sugar to her coffee.

I'm scared I might like this man.

Saturday 15 February

I've had my hair cut. The last time I had it done was after scattering Xavier's ashes at Cap de la Hague. I can't remember the name of the salon I went to near Barneville. I can't even remember the hairdresser's face. Anyway, it's pretty short … But I think that's a good thing. I asked Catherine to collect up the hair. She put it in a plastic bag for me. I burnt it on the fire.

Sunday 16 February

Nothing.

I shouldn't have cut my hair.

Monday 17 February

The bookshop's shut. Stupid me, I should have known. I'll go tomorrow.

Tuesday 18 February

I'll go tomorrow.

Wednesday 19 February

I've written so much that I'm almost at the end of my red notebook – I've even started writing on the inside of the back cover. But I only have a few lines to go. I'm sitting on a bench in the square. The two other booksellers have gone. Laurent hasn't locked the door. I can see him standing on a ladder at the back of the shop. This time, I'm going in.

Laurent glanced towards the door which had just opened with a tinkle. Using a pair of pliers and a cloth, he was attempting to fix the connection on a pipe which had leaked over a section of the paperbacks. It must have come loose when the water was switched back on a month ago. It had been slowly dripping, soaking the backs of the shelves without anyone noticing.

'Hello, I'm looking for a book ...'

'You've come to the right place,' replied Laurent, tightening up the copper band as firmly as he could.

'I don't know the author ...'

'Do you know what it's about?' Laurent tried instead, continuing to inspect the pipe. The band had nudged up a millimetre.

Laure took off her woolly hat and undid her scarf.

'It's the story of a bookseller who finds a handbag in the street one day, takes it home with him, empties out its contents and decides to look for the woman who owns it. He succeeds but when he finds her, he runs off like an idiot.'

Laurent froze on the ladder. Then, very slowly, he turned to look at her.

After a long silence, his heart thumping, he replied, 'We don't have that one, I'm afraid. In fact I don't think it's been written yet.'

The thing he had not dared expect but had hoped for all the same had happened: Laure Valadier had turned up in his bookshop. How on earth had she tracked him down? It didn't matter, she was here – and a lot of other things, like closing time or the leaky pipe, didn't matter either. Over her arm was the object that had kept him up at night for the last month. The object he knew by heart and which had in a sense become his. Laurent took a step down, then another and another until he was level with her. Those pale eyes were fixed on him, her hair was short now, and there was a knowing, enigmatic smile playing on her lips.

'I don't know what to say,' Laurent said quietly.

'Me neither,' said Laure, 'so I'll start at the beginning, with what everyone says when they meet for the first time.'

She lowered her eyes and then looked up at him.

'Hello, Laurent.'

The first sentence Laure Valadier wrote in her new red Moleskine notebook was: *I like kissing Laurent.*

This kiss took place forty-eight hours after their meeting, at the foot of Laure's building, in the exact same spot where the man had grabbed her bag five weeks earlier.

While she was closing her eyes and wrapping her arms around Laurent's back, five floors up Belphégor was clawing an armchair in the living room, just as Putin was doing four arrondissements away – it gave them both the same pleasurable feeling in their front paws.

At the moment Laurent was pulling Laure towards him, Pascal Masselou was adding three new female names to his 'Prospective' folder and noting a worrying 25.3 per cent decline in additions to the folder marked 'Stock'.

While Laure flicked the light switch in the entrance hall, Chloé was on MSN chatting online to a boy with glasses in the year above whose name was Alexandre and who, she had discovered one break time, shared her appreciation of the poems of Stéphane Mallarmé.

As the lift doors clattered shut on the fifth-floor landing, Frédéric Pichier was ripping up the first forty pages of the book he had been working on and finally resolving to write a modern-day novel: the story of a French literature teacher in a tough school and the brilliant career of one of his pupils, Djamila. He could not imagine that the idea forming in his mind would go on to win the Goncourt.

While Laure was unlocking the door, immediately letting the cat out onto the landing, William was sitting outside a café waiting for Julien, a past lover he hadn't seen for ten years and who had just got back in touch through Facebook. Watching him arrive, he told himself that perhaps Julien had been the one all along.

Three arrondissements away, with his fountain pen hovering above the page, Patrick Modiano had been debating for half an hour whether or not to put a comma after the first word of the last line of his new novel.

When Laurent and Laure fell onto the bed in the white bedroom, Patrick Modiano was still grappling with his punctuation conundrum. At the moment Laurent put his lips to her neck, Laure used her right foot to slip off her left ballet pump, which fell onto the parquet floor with a thud. Then she did the same with the other shoe. At the instant the second shoe landed on the same floorboard with the same sound, Patrick Modiano decided not to add a comma.